The Cocaine Princess 8

King Rio

**Lock Down Publications and Ca$h
Presents**
The Cocaine Princess 8
A Novel by *King Rio*

King Rio

Lock Down Publications
P.O. Box 944
Stockbridge, Ga 30281
www.lockdownpublications.com

Copyright 2023 by King Rio
The Cocaine Princess 8

First Edition March 2023
Printed in the United States of America

This is a work of fiction. Names, characters, places, and incidents either are products of the author's imagination or are used fictitiously. Any similarity to actual events or locales or persons, living or dead, is entirely coincidental.

Lock Down Publications
Like our page on Facebook: Lock Down Publications @
www.facebook.com/lockdownpublications.ldp
Book interior design by: **Shawn Walker**

4

Stay Connected with Us!

Text **LOCKDOWN** to 22828 to stay up-to-date with new releases, sneak peaks, contests and more…

Thank you!

King Rio

Submission Guideline.

Submit the first three chapters of your completed manuscript to ldpsubmissions@gmail.com, subject line: Your book's title. The manuscript must be in a .doc file and sent as an attachment. Document should be in Times New Roman, double spaced and in size 12 font. Also, provide your synopsis and full contact information. If sending multiple submissions, they must each be in a separate email.

Have a story but no way to send it electronically? You can still submit to LDP/Ca$h Presents. Send in the first three chapters, written or typed, of your completed manuscript to:

LDP: Submissions Dept
P.O. Box 944
Stockbridge, Ga 30281

DO NOT send original manuscript. Must be a duplicate.

Provide your synopsis and a cover letter containing your full contact information.

Thanks for considering LDP and Ca$h Presents.

Dedication

This book is dedicated to the readers. Every single one of you. Follow my new Facebook page: Author Rio (Author Rio Terrell page no longer in operation)

Twitter: authorrio Instagram: @authorrio5

If you are an avid reader of my books, the absolute best thing you can do for me is spread the word to your friends about my work.

Thank you and God bless. Enjoy the read!

King Rio

Prologue

"That's the guy who tried to kill your wife in Indianapolis," Enrique said, gesturing toward the severed head he'd just dropped on the floor in front of his wheelchair.

"Why in the fuck would you bring it here?!" Blake hopped out of bed, not even caring that he was stark naked, and grabbed his Glock off the nightstand.

"What kinda shit you on, Enrique? You can't be doing no shit like this. You see I got my lil chick laid up in here wit' me. How you gon' roll in here with a chopped off head and just throw the muhfucka on my marble floor?"

"I could care less about your side piece. Your wife's in the hospital, facing over four hundred federal indictments, and your sorry ass missed going to

see her because you've been too busy laying here fucking another woman." Enrique held up his left arm to show Blake the bandaged stomp where his left hand used to be.

"See that? I lost my fucking hand, for Christ's sake. Got burns all up and down my legs. This shit isn't fun."

Shaking his head in utter disbelief and pulling on a pair of fresh Versace boxers and True Religion jeans, Blake signaled for the girl in his bed — an Atlanta stripper he knew only as Baddie Barbie — to go into the bathroom. "Shut the door behind you."

She quickly ran to the bathroom and slammed the door closed.

The Hispanic woman in back of Enrique's wheelchair laughed, as if seeing a dead man's decapitated head being dropped to the floor was the most hilarious experience of her morning.

"You're the king of cocaine now," Enrique said. "Boss of the most powerful drug cartel in history. You'd better get ready to start seeing at least a couple of chopped off heads every day if you want to stay on top. There's no room for the timid in Mexico."

"Get the fuck out of my room," Blake snapped.

"Will do." Enrique's face was one big smile. "But before I go, I thought it best to tell you not to put Indianapolis on your travel list anytime soon.

Cops out there want you for questioning in a murder investigation."

The Hispanic lady behind Enrique pulled his wheelchair out of the doorway and disappeared down the hallway with him.

Blake stared at the head and tried to think of a way to dispose of it.

He also thought of the Indianapolis murder and hoped no eye-witnesses would be able to point him out as one of the gunmen.

"Oh, my God, Bulletface!" Barbie shouted from the bathroom. "What the hell?! That's a dead man's head!"

"He's definitely dead," Blake muttered vacantly.

Chapter 1

Tiffany "Tiff-Tiff" Jenkins had a secret. Well, her closest friends— Danielle, Tiesha, and Jessica— knew about it, but no one else did. It was a secret that she knew would make her an overnight celebrity if ever it was revealed. It had been the subject of conversation among her and her friends for the past few years. It was the source of every good dream she'd had since she'd first birthed Tim, her now 4-year-old son.

Reclined in the driver's seat of her Kia SUV with the door open and an ice-cold Pepsi in hand, listening to the soulful sounds of K. Michelle as the song blared from her speakers and acting like she was ignoring Danielle's half of a phone conversation, Tiff-Tiff had her eyes shut.

It was 7:18 pm.

"...Nuh uh, nigga, you steady likin' all that bitch's pictures on Facebook, then go and get some pussy from that hoe. I ain't got nothin' for yo' black ass... You know what, Lil Will? Fuck you. Stop calling my mothafuckin phone. Bye!"

"Girl," Tiffany said a few seconds later when she realized the call had ended, "I don't know why you put up with that nigga. You know he ain't shit."

"I'm done." Danielle lowered the music volume. "That nigga got me so fucked up it don't make no sense. I don't know who the fuck he think I am. Like I'm supposed to just let him stalk that hoe's page on FB without saying nothin'. Yeah right. He can get the fuck up out my house, that's what he can do."

Reluctantly, Tiffany opened her eyes and sighed. She was parked in front of the clapboard duplex home on the east side of Michigan City, Indiana, where she lived with J-Rock, her own no-good boyfriend. She'd caught him cheating with Christal, her whore of a neighbor, just last week. That incident had resulted in a one-night stand with the county jail and a $200 bond that J-Rock had paid out of his own pocket.

Now J-Rock was sitting on the concrete stairs of their front porch, smoking a blunt and watching Tim and Junior, Danielle's 3-year-old son, play with their remote control cars in the front yard.

There were a bunch of others outside on the block. Tiffany lived on East 10th Street, an area known for it's clique of drug-dealers and coke snorters. There were no big ballers, just low-level dope boys who mostly hustled to support their own habits, living among other 10th Street residents with menial low-income jobs that hardly paid enough to take care of home.

Tiffany was one of those menial workers. She was a manager at the local McDonald's. $37,000-a-year was enough to pay the bills, but it was nowhere close to where she wanted to be. She deserved more. She was a

bad bitch like her friend Danielle, a redbone with a nice body and a cute face who was wanted by just about every dope boy in the city.

But there was only one guy she wanted. Even if she couldn't have him, she could have his money. Or at least some of it. She knew this for certain.

"I need a nigga with some big money," Tiffany said. "I mean, yeah, J- Rock makes good money workin' at the club and sellin' weed, but it's not enough."

"Girl, who you tellin'? Will don't wanna do nothin' but smoke weed and snort powder all day. The nigga ain't even been helpin' out with the bills. I'm about to put his ass out today, watch."

"Yeah, right. He gon' eat the pussy and have yo' ass right back in love."

Danielle snickered and rubbed her generous thighs. "I need some good head right about now too."

Tiffany looked out her door as a white, '70's model Chevy Caprice convertible on large chrome rims came creeping past. It was a car she'd never seen in the neighborhood.

Suddenly, half of the guys and girls on the block began shouting, "Young! Wussup, Young!"

"Bitch, is that Courtney? Dub Life Young?" Danielle exclaimed.

Tiffany zoomed in on the Chevy's driver as he pulled over across the street and parked.

Sure enough, it was Young, a brown-skinned 4 Corner Hustler with dreadlocks who'd been in prison for the past ten years or so for a murder he'd committed on the west side of town.

"What the hell is that nigga doin' home? I thought he had life?" Tiffany said, more to herself than to Danielle.

"Nah, he only had like 25 years, I think. And you know they only gotta do like half. Plus the time cuts. Damn, he doin' good. That Chevy must've cost a grip."

"Yeah?" Tiffany's eyes had yet to stray from the box Chevy. She watched Young step out, and as soon as she saw him— dressed in an expensive- looking outfit and spiked Louboutin sneakers— she knew she had to have him.

Luck was on her side.

Just then, J-Rock's brother Reggie pulled up in his rust-laden Tahoe to take J-Rock to work at Joffy's, a new nightclub his uncle owned downtown.

Tiffany gave J-Rock a quick peck on the lips before hopping in the SUV with his brother and leaving.

"Come on, bitch," Tiffany said, and stepped out to the street.

She waved for Young, knowing he'd remember her. When he looked her way, he smiled and walked toward her. He had on the silly expression she remembered him by, and his smile was captivating. He looked basically the same as he'd looked when she'd last seen him, just much heavier and tatted up.

He made it to her and gave her a hug.

"Tiff-Tiff and Danielle," he said, hugging Danielle. "Damn, I never thought I'd see y'all again. How y'all been?"

"I'm good," Tiffany said. "I just got done cooking. You hungry?"

He smirked. "Hell yeah. You see this stomach, nigga. I ain't turnin' nothin' down. I just got out, a nigga need some good food."

"I see yo' fat ass been eatin'," Danielle said and laughed.

He turned to her with his brows furrowed. "Awwww...you got jokes?

That's why yo' face look like —"

"Okay, okay, I quit," Danielle said, raising her hands in defeat before he could go all in.

He and Tiffany laughed.

"Make me get on yo' ass." He chuckled, obviously ready to roast her at any given moment.

"Come on." Tiffany turned and headed up the walkway to her

13

front door.

She shouted an order to the boys to follow her inside and play in Tim's room.

Danielle knitted her brows at Tiffany. They had just left Taco Bell a half hour prior because Tiff hadn't felt like cooking dinner; no one had cooked this evening.

Tiffany was up to something.

In the house, Tiffany led Young to her bedroom. Danielle shadowed them into the room, smiling widely.

"When did you come home?" Tiffany asked as Young sat down at the foot of her queen size bed.

"This past Sunday. I been home five days. Shit, I'm glad you cooked, I was just on my way to grab me somethin' to eat." His eyes fell on Tiffany's 50-inch widescreen television. J-Rock had left his PlayStation 4 paused on a Grand Theft Auto 5 mission. "Nigga, is this..."

"It's GTA 5," Tiffany said. "Let me go and warm up you a plate. You eat tacos? I made some nachos and hardshell tacos. Tastes just like Taco Bell." She cracked a smirk and gave Danielle a wink.

Danielle rolled her eyes and returned the smirk.

Young was already picking up the PlayStation controller. "Yeah, I eat all dat shit. Man, I fucks wit' this game. Been wantin' to play this muhfucka since it came out. I'm goin' to get it tomorrow."

Tiffany sent Danielle to warm up the tacos and nachos and bring the food to the bedroom while she herself sat on the bed and popped the top on a fifth of Hennessy that had been sitting on her bedside table.

"You drink?" she asked.

"Yeah." Young nodded. "Not tonight, though, I gotta get home." "You can stay the night here. My nigga don't get off until six in the

morning. As long as you leave before then you can stay."

Young pressed pause on the game and looked back at Tiff with a knowing smile. He laughed. "Lemme find out you hoes tryna buss me down tonight."

Out of the corner of her eye, Tiffany saw that he was staring at

14

her. She filled a glass with cognac and shouted for Danielle to bring three cups of ice.

"So," she asked, "you got a girl? I remember you used to fuck around with J."

"I ain't got no girl. I'm fresh out the joint, ain't lettin' none of these lil thots out here lock me down."

"Hmm." Tiffany wanted to ask how he'd been able to buy such expensive clothes but decided against it for now. She'd definitely ask later, though.

When Danielle came in with the food, they ate in silence for a couple of minutes before Tiffany hit him with two more questions.

"How'd you get that car? Is it yours?" "Hell yeah, that's my shit. I just bought it."

"You had that money saved up from before you went to jail?"

"Nah, my nigga sent me fifty racks. You know Blake a billionaire now.

That's my lil nigga. Told me to just ask him if I needed any—"

The sudden, harsh shriek of Danielle screaming silenced Young and compelled Tiffany's eyes to widen in horror. She looked at the door just as Danielle was shoved into the bedroom...by someone in a ski-mask who had a black revolver aimed at Danielle's back.

He was chubby and his dark blue Pacers hoodie was as dirty as his jeans and sneakers. His eyes darted around the room, searching.

"Where the fuck is that nigga Blake's baby—" the masked man started. He never got another word out.

Young snatched a pistol from his hip and opened fire. BOOM BOOM BOOM BOOM BOOM BOOM BOOM.

Danielle and Tiffany screamed until the gunshots ceased. At least two rounds had plowed through the masked gunman's face, and the others had struck his chest and knocked blood out of his back and onto the hallway wall across from the bedroom door.

By the time the gunman hit the tan-colored carpet, Young was stepping over the corpse with his gun— a .40-caliber Glock, Tiffany noticed, with an extended clip and red laser sighting— raised and ready to fire.

Instinctively, Tiffany and Danielle raced out of the room and up the hall to Tim's bedroom where they found their two little boys kneeled down at Tim's toy box, eyes wide and frightened. They stared up at their mothers as their hands were grabbed and they were yanked to their feet.

"Y'all, come on," Young shouted from the living room. Tiffany and Danielle were at his side a moment later.

They made it to the front porch just in time to see an orange Hummer on oversized rims appear from around the corner of 10th and Lafayette and speed off down the block.

Half of the neighborhood had apparently hauled ass at the sound of gunfire because the previously crowded street was now practically empty.

Tiffany and Danielle rushed toward the SUV with their children. "What the fuck, man," Danielle said in disbelief. "What the fuck just

happened? I was on my way to the bedroom when that dude busted in the door with his gun out. What was he saying?"

"Somebody's been running their mouth to the wrong people." Tiffany buckled the boys into the backseat and turned to face Danielle. "He said 'Where is Blake's baby?', so I know somebody talked. It's not like Blake knows Tim is his son."

Chapter 2
O'Hare International Airport, Chicago

There weren't many black men who could stand toe to toe with Blake "Bulletface" King when it came to net worths. Out of Hip Hop's top five wealthiest men, he was #1 with $1.27 billion, followed by Dr. Dre with
$810 million, Diddy with $700 million, Jay Z with $650 million, and Master P with $350 million.

In addition to being the reigning king of the rap game, he was also the king of the drug trade, thanks to his marriage to the boss of Mexico's most lucrative drug cartel, the one and only Alexus Costilla. She was currently in a coma in a Los Angeles hospital, handcuffed to her bed and facing hundreds of federal indictments. Her hospitalization made Blake the stand- in boss of the cartel, a position that he took seriously.

With well over $800 million of his own drug money stashed throughout the many homes he owned across the United States, he had no choice but to take his secondary job as the cocaine king as serious as he took the rap game.

He was essentially the boss of all bosses, and he had to admit, being number-one certainly had its perks.

For one, he could afford the millions of dollars in jewelry that graced his neck and wrists every day and night, and the tens of thousands of dollars in singles that he rained on strippers every weekend. He could afford the matte black, armored 2016 Mercedes Maybach S600 that Remo, his driver, was now pulling away from the airport in, and the Boeing 747 that had transported it here behind his Gulfstream 650 jet. The curvaceous 21-year- old stripper in the backseat next to him was a dime piece yellowbone with a waterfall of raven hair and an ass out of this world, and he knew that he would've never had a chance with her had he been broke. He'd taken her shopping on Collins Avenue in Miami Beach before boarding his private jet and heading to Chicago; she was now looking the part of a well-off side chick in a curve-hugging Gucci dress and matching heels. He'd paid for her mani and pedi, her brand-new Gucci bag, and the white diamond Rolex watch on her slender left wrist.

"Fucked up your wife is in the hospital all burnt up like that,"

Barbie said, eyeing her perfectly done fingernails from behind a pair of Gucci sunglasses.

"She'll be good," Blake replied. "I'll go and see her when she comes out of that coma, get everything situated."

The only thing on his mind now was the drug shipment the Costilla Cartel had coming in this afternoon. 8,000 kilos of Colombian cocaine. He would sell the kilos to mob bosses and dealers in over eighty cities in 24 states for

$16,000 apiece and clear $128 million this month without ever having

touched a single gram. Another shipment would be delivered to the Mexican Mafia members who'd been moving the cartel's dope for years.

Another $158 million would be made off that deal.

He eye-fucked Barbie's meaty thighs and sipped from his Styrofoam cup of "Prometh with Codeine" and Sprite on ice. He was dressed in an all- black Versace outfit with Louboutin sneakers and a black-and-gold Louis Vuitton belt that coincided with the gold and yellow-diamond jewelry on his neck and wrists and his diamond-encrusted gold teeth.

Two iPhones were on his lap, but he had both of them on airplane mode, and for now they'd stay that way. He had an assistant — Kendall Ashland, a girl he'd met near the Versace Mansion a few years prior— whose phone would automatically be forwarded his unanswered calls. She was way out in Calabasas, California, waiting on him to get there early tomorrow.

"So," Barbie asked, "you and Alexus just happened to break up right before some bitch detonated a suicide bomb in front of her and Mercedes?"

"Ain't that what I told you?" Blake hated questions.

"Niggas tell bitches a lot of shit. Don't always mean it's true."

"What the fuck I gotta lie for?"

She shrugged.

"I ain't got no reason to lie," he said, adjusting his icy watch. "It ain't like I'm tryna wife you, anyway. I'm staying single now. Fuck a relationship. I want a new bitch every now and then. I'm tired of relationships."

This seemed to bother Barbie; she gave him a funny look and

18

went on silent mode for the next twenty minutes or so.

He took advantage of the quiet spell and checked his smartphones. He had an album release party to attend tonight. His newest addition to Money Bagz Management, Biggs, was celebrating the release of his debut album, arrogantly titled "Rich Already". It featured some of the hottest artists in the industry and even a few newbies, like Fetty Wap and Dej Loaf. The two songs on the album that featured Bulletface — "Drill Season" and "All O' Dat"— were currently among the most-requested songs on the radio. "Drill Season" was the #1 bestseller on iTunes' list of bestselling rap songs.

He dialed up Biggs on one iPhone while scrolling through his Instagram notifications on the other.

"Yoooo," Biggs answered. "What up, Lord. You in the city?"

"Yep, just landed. On my way to the Highland Park spot in a few. Y'all there yet?

"Nigga, everybody and they momma here. Fuck you thought? This our year, and this my city. You know I brought every bad bitch in Chicago out. Lanipop here, too. She say she can't wait to meet you. "

Blake smiled widely. Lanipop was a stripper he'd wanted to fuck since before he'd gotten famous and became a billionaire. She was thick and tatted up, as pretty as can be, and all about her money, three qualities that he'd always loved in a woman.

"Dej and Durk just showed up, too," Biggs continued. "Durk wants you on that Remember My Name album he about to drop."

"Yeah?" Blake nodded to himself. "Facetime me, bruh." "Yep."

Seconds later Blake was looking at the many faces of the celebrities who'd already arrived at his Highland Park mansion. Biggs twisted and turned the phone in every direction. Lanipop waved and shouted a hello, and so did several dozen other scantily clad models and strippers. Sicko Mobb, Do or Die, Twista, Shawnna, Da Brat, Dreezy, and a number of other Chicago rap artists were also present.

"I told you," Biggs said, smiling like always as his face filled the screen. "Shit real, bruh. We T'd up all day for this album release. We got catered soul food, two hundred bottles of Ace, strippers. And we both single. Can't beat it."

Blake chuckled. Biggs had broken up with Mercedes Costilla

mere seconds before Blake had called it quits with Alexus.

"I'm on my way now, bruh," Blake sipped some Lean. "Yup, Mighty," Biggs said and hung up.

Conversation ceased for a long moment. Barbie's thumbs skittered across her smartphone screen as she composed a tweet. Blake uploaded a pic of Biggs's album cover with the caption "Biggs still goin' hard, nigga! #RichAlready the album! #MBM #ThePowerCircle"

When the upload was complete, he added another pic, this one of himself standing in the hallway of The Versace Mansion wearing a black and gold Louis Vuitton robe and holding a gold-plated AK-47 in one hand and a Kush-stuffed blunt and a Styrofoam of Lean in the other. $2 million in bank-new hundreds was piled up around his Louis Vuitton sneakers on the white marble floor. He captioned it "#KingShit #MBM #ThisOurSummer"

Barbie shattered the silence. "Who the fuck is Lanipop?"

"That's my business, ain't it?"

She sucked her teeth indignantly and rolled her eyes. "Boy, I cannot believe I'm actually sitting here with you. You don't know how jealous bitches would be of me if they knew I was with you. I should post a pic of us."

"No the fuck you shouldn't." Blake chuckled and shook his head. "Alexus is still my wife. They'll kill you before the sun sets."

"Boy, do I look like I'm worried about what a bitch think about me? So what she's Alexus."

"Yeah, a'ight. You just don't know. Alexus and her family ain't to be played with. Pedro just bonded out, too. He'll send somebody to blow your head off as soon as the pic is released. Not to mention the fact that it would be all over TMZ and World Star asap. Nah, let's just keep this between us for a while."

Barbie gave him another suck of the teeth and roll of the eyes. Her mannerisms were so sexy to Blake. She was one of the prettiest girls he had ever dated, and the fact that her sex game matched her snide attitude attracted him to her like a moth to a flame.

He eased toward her and planted a kiss on her cheek. She at-

20

tempted to shy away from his lips but he grabbed the back of her neck and and kept his mouth pressed to her face.

He set his Styrofoam in the cup holder, swiped his iPhones off his lap, and pulled her to him. Her big ass felt amazingly soft as it slid onto his lap. He kissed at the nape of her neck, then she turned and pressed her equally soft lips against his for a long moment.

"Is this just a fling or do you see us being a couple one day?" she asked. "Let's take it one day at a time."

His right hand disappeared under her dress. He caressed her hairless pussy until she moaned an mmmm and kissed him again. This time she sucked on his bottom lip.

"You know what I like?" he said. "Better yet, do you know what I love?"

The rightside of her mouth rose in a salacious smirk. "I'm guessing it has something to do with this hard thing I'm feeling under my ass."

"You must be a psychic." Blake displayed his blinging diamond grin. His index and middle fingers slipped into Barbie's wet pussy.

Both his smartphones jangled to life in unison. He glanced at them, intent on ignoring the calls.

But on one phone Biggs was calling again, and on the other his guy Young, who'd just recently gotten out of prison, was calling back.

"One second, baby," he said to Barbie as he answered Young's call. "Bruh...this Bee Kay?"

"Naw, it's Kay Bee," Blake said sarcastically and laughed. "What's up, bruh?"

"Bruh, shit just went down at Tiff-Tiff crib. I had just came in the bedroom with her and Danielle, bruh. Some nigga walked in with a strap and a mask on asking for your baby. I stanked the nigga. On Angelo.

Following the hoes to Tiff-Tiff's momma's crib now."

Blake took half a minute to think; then, "Bruh, whose gun did you use?" "My brother's."

"Quez?"

"Yeah, nigga, how many muhfuckin brothers I got?"

"Clean the strap off and give it to Tiff. Tell her to tell the law Quez is her nigga and she had his gun in her purse. When the nigga busted in the door, she upped it and started blowin'. And tell her don't say nothing else after that. I'll get her a lawyer if she needs one. Just make sure you don't tell them you shot that nigga. We can't have you going back to the joint, bruh."

"I wonder why he came in asking for your baby?" Young said. "Maybe he was talkin' about another Blake."

"Ain't no tellin'. Bruh, come to Chicago. Get on the highway now. Biggs got his album release party tonight at the Jordan mansion. All kinds of rich niggas and bad bitches in there T'd up for us. It's still Dub Life or no life, nigga, ain't shit changed. And fuck that nigga, whoever he was. Bring Tiff and Danielle with you. I'll reimburse you when y'all get here and send em shoppin' for some new clothes for the party."

"Tiff wanna go to the police station first. The law already at her house. I'm saying I wasn't even there. I'll hitchoo when I get to the city, bruh. Dub Life, nigga."

"Or no life, nigga."

Blake ended the call and picked up his Styrofoam and sipped, gazing out his window as his sleek black Maybach smoothly traversed the mildly congested Eisenhower traffic. Every driver that passed stared at his car, not knowing that its owner was a billionaire rap star who was vicariously responsible for just about every gram of heroin and cocaine in the city.

Seemingly upset by Blake's sudden shift in attention, Barbie sucked her teeth and went back to her seat, pinching the bottom of her dress between thumb and forefinger and pulling it down to her knees.

He shook his head, grinning.

"I'll take care of you when we get in the mansion," he said.

"Don't say 'take care' of me, like I'm some kind of sex-addicted nympho." Barbie bit the corner of her bottom lip and smirked at him. Remo was pulling to a stop in front of the Highland Park estate, a mansion Blake had purchased for close to $30 million from Michael Jordan years ago. It still had the number 23 on the wrought-iron gates. The 32,000-square-foot home consisted of nine bedrooms, fifteen bathrooms, a full basketball court, an indoor swimming pool, an outdoor tennis court, and a driving range.

"You're addicted already," Blake accused. "Yeah, right. It was good but it wasn't all that." "You didn't say that shit in Cali." "Whatever."

The gate opened slowly, and Remo drove up to the mansion. The driveway was replete with foreign cars. Blake's two-million-dollar Newell tour bus stood tall between Biggs's Ferrari and Young Meach's Rolls-Royce Wraith.

Instead of waiting on Remo to open her door, Barbie pushed it open herself and stepped out of the pricey Mercedes. Her bountiful derrière made a wedgie of the back of her dress, and seeing her yank it free compelled Blake to reach out a hand to squeeze it, but she slammed the door shut on him and smiled in through the window.

Getting out of the car, he returned the missed call from Biggs.

"Bruh," Biggs said, and Blake could immediately tell that something was wrong. "I just got word. Some BD's from Parkway Gardens got some money on you. They say if you don't break bread they on gunplay. Durk tryna figure out what that shit's all about now."

Blake dropped his head back and chuckled. "Nigga, I was born for that shit. I'm outside now, bruh. Let the games begin."

King Rio

Chapter 3

Mexico

Pedro Costilla sat quietly at the bar with his head down inside Steel 33, wearing a white Hartmarx suit with a thin, gold silk tie. The glass on the countertop in front of him was half full of cognac on ice. After having just dropped $23 million to bail out of jail on numerous federal indictments, and having many of his properties and vehicles seized in the drug raids that had led to his arrest, Pedro was a nervous wreck.

He was in Juarez, the infamous city in Mexico's state of Chihuahua. Once known as the world's most dangerous city, Ciudad Juarez was a lot calmer these days. Just a few years prior the city had recorded a staggering 3,255 murders; this year so far there had only been 270 murders, mostly because the Sinaloa and Juarez cartels that had been engaged in a bloody war had joined forces with the Costilla Cartel. Alexus, their new boss, wanted peace and prosperity instead of war, and that's exactly what she was getting.

There were two college-age girls — one an attractive Latina in ripped jeans and a halter top, the other a skinny Black girl in a fuchsia sundress — sitting to the left of him, and a burly, foul-smelling behemoth of a man to his right. He'd seen the guy around Juarez on numerous occasions, and every time the man was drunk and disorderly. The people called him Vodka; it's all he ever drank, and the potent scent of it lingered whenever he was around.

"Hey...you..."

A sudden poke in his left side made Pedro raise his head and look toward the voice.

It was the girl closest to him, the Latina. He knew from listening to their conversation that her name was Lisa and her friend's name was Mary.

Her and Mary wore concerned expressions on their pretty faces. Lisa's drink was gone and she had an inebriated slur to her voice.

"Aren't you, like, Alexus's cousin or something?" Lisa asked.

He just looked at her and said nothing. The four dark-clothed bodyguards assigned to protecting him were standing directly behind him, each facing a different direction. Their guns were concealed but their cantankerous scowls weren't. All the locals knew Pedro well.

Apparently, the two girls were not in the know.

"We're from El Paso," Lisa continued. "Well, we live there. I'm actually from Kansas City. Mary's from Indianapolis. We go to the same school. You ever been to El Paso? It's right over the border, just a hop and a skip away."

Mary intervened: "We were going to ask if Flako Costilla was your father.

We saw on the news that his body was found floating in the Rio Grande."

Pedro's wise green eyes shifted to the Black girl. He studied her flawless visage for a brief moment.

"Yes," he said finally, "Flako was my father. But he was never a real Costilla. Good riddance."

Lisa gasped and clamped both hands over her mouth. Her eyes widened.

Pedro wondered what the hell she was so shocked about.

When she lowered her hands a second later he found out.

"You're related to... Oh, my God. Are you a billionaire, too? That means Alexus really is your cousin! Jesus fucking Christ!" She shot a glance at Mary. "You were right!"

Suddenly enthused, Pedro eased back on the barstool, smiling broadly, and shouted for the bartender. "Drinks on me tonight," he said. "All night long."

These were the nights that Vodka enjoyed. He was the first on his feet to cheer and order two shots of the very best vodka Steel 33 had to offer.

The bar became packed almost instantly, so much so that Pedro's bodyguards grew frustrated and shoved several men away from their boss. Lisa excused herself to the restroom amid all the confusion. As Mary took her friend's stool, Pedro dug in the pocket of his slacks and withdrew two ten-thousand-dollar packets of hundred-dollar bills.

"I assume you're familiar with the American dollar." He glanced at a tattoo on Mary's wrist as she nodded her head and cast a knowing smirk at him. It read 'Ghost G' in blue cursive letters that were written over a heart. His eyes ascended to hers. "Is he a black guy?"

She frowned. "Who?"

Again he looked at the tattoo.

"Oh," she said with a light giggle. "Yeah. My ex." He's from Chicago, in prison now but he'll be home next month. He was heavy into all that gang stuff in Chicago. The Gangster Disciples. He's promising to leave it all alone now. I don't know. I told him we're done."

She shrugged her narrow shoulders and picked up her glass of cognac. It was full; she'd hardly taken a sip. Her fingernails were painted the same shade of pink as her heels and leather Chanel bag. Her hair— short and black with pink highlights — was shoulder length and as straight as a

paper's edge. She had a cute face, a thin nose, and full lips that were also coated in pink glossy lipstick.

"Still love him?" Pedro asked. Another shrug.

"Why are you in Juarez?" he prodded. "It's dangerous here."

"Not as dangerous as it used to be," she reasoned. "And besides, what's life without a little danger, you know? We came here to visit Lisa's uncle, anyway. Just for the night. We'll be back home first thing tomorrow."

Pedro nodded his head and peeled four crisp Benjamins from the stack of cash. He laid them next to Mary's glass.

"You come with me, and I'll guarantee you a safe trip home. Like I said, it's not safe here." He fingered a curlicue of hair from over her eye, leaning closer in an attempt to inhale her scent. He knew it would be a pleasant perfume, and indeed it was.

"What's the money for?" she asked. Her question went unanswered.

Just then, a piercing scream resounded through the building. It came from near the restrooms.

In Spanish, someone shouted, "They're taking her!"

Instinctively, Mary hopped down from the barstool and headed through the crowd toward the restrooms. Pedro snatched up the cash he'd given her and followed her, elbowing people aside and drawing his gold-plated .50- caliber Desert Eagle from the shoulder holster under his left arm. His men pushed ahead of him and made it easier for him and Mary to reach the hallway where the restrooms and a rear exit were located.

27

There were two men rushing out of the exit behind a third man who was dragging Lisa out into the dark alleyway by her hair.

When Pedro's men drew their Tec-9 submachine guns, all three of the men froze.

"Let go of her!" Mary demanded. Pedro did not hesitate.

He shot one of the men dead with a carefully aimed headshot. His bodyguards opened fire on the other man, leaving only the guy holding Lisa gawking in fear and sending the bar's patrons stampeding out of the front doors.

"Pedro Costilla!" said the man who was holding Lisa. "Listen, we—" BOOM.

Another .50-caliber round exploded from Pedro's golden gun.

Half the guy's head departed from the rest of it and landed with a sickening thud on the gravel behind him. Lisa screamed, fell to her hands and knees, and crawled hurriedly to Mary.

Two minutes later Pedro and the two American girls were in the back seats of his blacked-out luxury Escalade. Two more identical SUVs were parked behind it.

He told his driver to head for the border.

Chapter 4

'Hit the Lambo dealership, fuck one whip I bought all o' dat
Papi said he had a thousand bricks, I said fuck it let me get all
o' dat Left Magic City wit a bad bitch, I fucked her once I ain't
callin' back Think I'm all o' dat wit this bag o' chips, big bags o'
chips I got all o' dat If I'm in the city it's snowstormin'
Guns blowin' ain't no warnings Got big heaters... global war-
min'
Hit Caper up for dat Glo performance My niggas wit me dem
poles be on em They come wit me all da hoes be on em
We got all the guns, all the dope, all the diamonds, and all the
money Money Bagz, billionaires, yeah we in this bitch till the roof
burnin' Got twin forties...and twin K's
That's stovetop, I got fo' burnas Man, I need me a bad bitch
Tell her count the bag while I get the dough From doin' shows
and sellin' coke
The gang shit dat my fellas on...
There was so much Kush smoke in the air that Blake found it
difficult to see more than a few feet ahead of him.

Mostly everyone was crowded around the indoor swimming
pool, and the few that weren't were in the pool with two dozen
strippers and models Biggs had invited to the party. Large, twenty-
thousand-dollar bottles of Ace were being passed around the room,
as were blunts and pills and everything else the guests had brought
along to brighten their night. Many guests were seated along the
custom white leather sofa that stretched along the walls.

Some were on the lounge chairs that encircled the pool. A lot
of them had
brought in catered barbecue from the kitchen down the hall. A
few strippers were twerking to the bass of Biggs's "All O' Dat",
which had Blake on the hook as well as the third verse.

Blake, Biggs, and Young Meach were holding down the center
of the sofa with big blunts and Styrofoams full of Lean. Glock
handguns with 30-round magazines lay in their laps. They all wore
heavy gold and diamond chains with blinging MBM pendants.

Like many of the girls, Barbie had drank a little too much. She
and Lanipop had shed their dresses long ago and were now sitting
beside each other on the marble edge of the swimming pool, both

staring in his direction with seductive smiles on their flawless faces.

"Them hoes over there plottin'," Meach guessed aloud. He nudged an elbow in Blake's side. "Don't trust them hoes, bruh. You know how grimey bitches be, especially them stripper hoes."

"You think I'm goin' for anything?" Blake asked, blowing out a stream of smoke. "I can't trust myself. The fuck I look like trustin' a bitch? You know what I'm on wit' em."

"Yeah," Biggs said, "and you know what they on witchoo."

Biggs was right. Every girl in America wanted a piece of Bulletface. To women, he was a sex symbol like 50 Cent and LL. Only he was a lot wealthier and a whole lot more gangster than anyone in Hip Hop history. He had been in more murder and shooting investigations than any rapper ever— in fact, he was currently under scrutiny by the Indianapolis Metropolitan Police Department for a double murder on the city's west side. But he was filthy rich and getting richer by the day, and all the ladies wanted was a piece of the American dream he was living. If they were lucky they'd get a ring and a baby out of him, but all would settle for just the latter if they could, knowing that the child alone would generate enough revenue to take care of both child and mother.

Blake didn't really care. He had enough money to go around. Child support was nothing compared to the many joys of fatherhood. He'd welcome another baby with open arms, add another King to his legacy.

One of his iPhones lit up as he was grinning back at Barbie and Lanipop.

It was Young, calling to say he'd just pulled up outside at the gate. Blake waved for the older Mexican lady who'd been his personal butler since he bought the place and sent her to see Young in.

"Man, I'm so glad to see Young home," Meach said. His hair was short and wavy like Blake's.

They shated "Now all we need is Lil Lord and we'll be good. Back to the day one Dub Life niggas."

"If bruh come home," Biggs said, "it's gon' be hell in the streets. You already know he whackin' niggas off top. Shit, he got court next week. He might be home sooner than we think."

Blake shrugged and sipped and smoked some more. His attention went to Nona, Biggs's sister, as she came sauntering over to him in a one-piece swimsuit.

She was Blake's ex-girlfriend, a curvaceous, yellowish-brown-skinned urban model who'd graced the covers of every Hip Hop magazine in the game, mostly due to her fame from being one of the few models Bulletface had dated.

She stood before him with globules of water dripping down her body, hands planted on her tiny waistline, eyes fixed on the king.

"Boy." She always spoke to him this way; he enjoyed it. "When am I going to get the side chick treatment like that new bitch you done started fuckin'? I see she smilin' all in ya face. You in love with the bitch already? And why y'all got guns out? Ain't we celebrating my brother's —"

In a flash, Biggs got up and lifted Nona high in the air. She gasped and slapped the top of his head.

"Biggs, if you throw me in that —"

But she was soaring into the swimming pool before she could complete the threat.

Laughing with the gang, Blake got to his feet, putting the Glock in the Louis Vuitton holster under his left arm and holding his Styrofoam as Young came walking in ahead of Tiff-Tiff and Danielle.

Instinctively, Blake looked around the room to count the women he'd slept with in the past. Lakita "Bubbles" Thomas, another of Chicago's more popular strippers, was at the wet bar with her friend Shay and Durk's OTF crew; Blake had bedded Bubbles on and off for the past four years or so.

The best sex he'd ever had — aside from his wife— was with Tiff-Tiff.

She had that tight, warm, gushy pussy that niggas killed for.

He hugged her tight when she made it to him, smiling over her shoulder at Nona's angry face as she climbed out of the pool.

"I'm so fucking scared right now," Tiff said, pulling back to look at Blake. "Some nigga done ran up in my house when my baby was there. Now the

police think I killed him in self-defense. This shit is crazy."

"You'll be a'ight." Blake have her lower back a comforting rub. "Stay the night here with me. I got nine bedrooms in this bitch. Shit, I need some guests. I'll pay for your lawyer if you need one, too. Matter of fact, I'm gon' get Britney on top of it first thing in the morning. You ain't got no worries, a'ight?"

He kissed her on the forehead. Her face lit up.

"Bruh," Meach said, draping an arm around Blake's shoulder, "let's get in traffic. This party done for. We need to be slidin' on them niggas that got that money on yo' head."

Blake shook his head no. His eyes were on Tiff's barely-there shorts. He could clearly see the print off her plump pussy through the crotch of the shorts, and her braless nipples were poking out of her shirt. She'd gotten a bit thicker since he last saw her. Prettier, too.

Or was it the Lean and Kush playing tricks on him? He wasn't sure.

Biggs stayed to send everyone home while Blake and the gang led Tiff and Danielle out into the hallway and to the elevator that would take them up to the second-floor bedroom they'd be sleeping in. While they walked, Tiffany and Young gave him more details on what had happened at her place in Michigan City.

They were at the guest bedroom door when Danielle said something that stopped Blake in his tracks.

"Some nigga sped off in a burnt orange Hummer," Danielle said. "We're guessing he was the getaway driver."

"A burnt orange Hummer?" Blake couldn't believe it. "On thirties? Some big ass rims?"

Tiff and Danielle nodded their heads in unison. Blake became thoughtful.

He pushed open the bedroom door and preceded them into the lavishly furnished room. The floor boasted expensive white fur rugs and carpeting in some places and gleaming white marble in others. The heavy white blanket on the king-size bed was custom Versace. A 70-inch Smart TV with surround sound hung on the wall across from the bed.

"Make yourselves at home," Blake said. "Just hit this intercom button on the wall whenever you need the maids or the butler. They'll come right up.

I'm sending the maids and my butler up to take care of any-thing y'all need now. I'll be right down the hall in my bedroom."

Tiff-Tiff stuck out her bottom lip in an obvious pout. Blake grinned as he and the guys left the room.

"She wanna fuck, bruh," Young said as soon as the door was closed. "That bitch want some dick."

"Fuck all dat." Blake's expression turned serious. "The Hummer y'all saw leaving Tiff's crib. It's T-Walk's brothers."

Meach shook his head. "Can't be them. V-Walk and B-Walk sittin' in the county jail."

"It's somebody they sent." Blake started down the hallway, thinking of a way to figure out what was going on. "They had somethin' to do with it. All we gotta do is find out who they gave the Hummer keys to, who's been driving it. Can't be that hard. Bright ass Hummer on some big dumb ass rims. A nigga can't miss that."

Barbie, Bubbles, and Nona rounded the corner up ahead. They were drying off with towels and laughing about something. Bubbles waved at Blake when she saw him.

All three of the girls were strippers with huge derrières and pretty faces.

Seeing their asses and thighs wobble and bounce as they walked toward him made Blake temporarily forget all about the orange Hummer.

"Hey, Bulletface." Lakita "Bubbles" Thomas's voice was soft and sweet. "Hey, Kita." Blake grinned.

Barbie sucked her teeth and squinted at him. All attitude. They'd hardly known each other two days and already she was becoming territorial.

He didn't even know the girl's real name, for Christ's sake. "Where's your bedroom?" Barbie asked. "We're trying to get in the shower. And they wanna stay the night with us."

"Sure," Blake said quickly, showing his diamond-encrusted golds in a winning grin. "Feel free." He pointed to the door at the end of the hall. "That's it right there."

"Thank yoooou," Bubbles cooed as they sauntered past the guys.

Blake turned to the gang with a shit-eating grin. "I'll catch up wit' y'all niggas later."

"Bullshit," Young said, chuckling. "Nigga, if you about to kick it with them, I'm about to chill with Danielle and Tiff."

"Man, I'm good," Meach said, turning to leave. "I got a bad bitch in the pool waitin' on me now. Biggs got her buddy. We might fuck them hoes by the pool."

Young was already on his way into the bedroom with Tiff and Danielle by the time Meach rounded the corner.

Looking back over his shoulder, Blake saw that his own bedroom door was just closing. He got a chance to glimpse the replica of Gucci Mane's ice cream tattoo on Nona's left butt cheek before the door closed.

"Fuck it," he muttered, and started off toward his bedroom.

As he was passing the guest bedroom where Tiff and Danielle were staying, Tiffany opened it a crack and stuck her head out.

"The guy Young killed," she said. "He asked for your baby right before Young shot him."

Blake frowned. "My baby?" "Yeah."

"Why would he think my baby was there?"

Tiff-Tiff sighed, stepped out of the bedroom, and shut the door behind her.

Blake's frown deepened.

"Remember when we fucked at Dawn's Christmas party," she said, slipping her fingers into the front pockets of her blue jean short-shorts, "the night you got shot up the first time? Well, I got pregnant, and at first I thought the baby was Tim-Tim's, because he was my boyfriend at the time. But we got a DNA test and he wasn't the father."

"So, you're saying —"

"You know what the fuck I'm sayin'. You the only nigga I fucked other than Tim. My son is your son."

34

Chapter 5

Lisa was sobbing weakly, sitting on Mary's lap like a distraught child with her head on Mary's shoulder.

Pedro popped a bottle of Dom Perignon 1959 Vintage champagne and poured himself a glass. His cool green eyes fluctuated between the two young women and the 46-inch curved television that separated them from the driver and front passenger, two highly trained cartel bodyguards who'd been watching over Pedro for nearly a decade.

As usual, Pedro was watching episodes of Breaking Bad, his favorite show. He'd watched and rewatched every season several times since the

finale first aired last year. Seeing the disturbed old school teacher cooking up and dealing meth never failed to bring a smile to the cartel lieutenant's face.

"You don't seem too upset about that shooting," Mary commented.

Pedro scoffed at her comment. "Upset? Upset for what? The bastards got what they deserved. They were going to take her and sell her to a rich Mexican drug runner. He would have used her to his liking, chopped up her body, and buried it on the side of the road somewhere in Juarez. I've been doing business here since I was a kid. I've seen it happen too many times to count on all my fingers and toes."

"You still...you know. You shot them. That doesn't bother you?"

"No." Pedro picked up the TV remote control and lowered the volume. His driver was just crossing the border.

"Let's say we stop for a quick bite," Pedro suggested. "The Good Luck Café. One of the best restaurants in all of El Paso. It's right down on Alameda, a four or five minute drive from here."

He looked at Mary, ignoring Lisa, whose head was shaking in disagreement.

"I'm stopping there. You two don't have to eat," Pedro said.

"She'll wanna eat later. We've been to Good Luck before. A friend of mine used to work there. I'm hungry, anyway."

"Good Luck, it is." Pedro ordered his driver to head for the restaurant. "I left the money you gave me on the counter at that bar," Mary said. "Yeah, I know." He dug in his pocket and fished out the four hundred- dollar bills. He straightened them up, for they had gained a few crinkles.

"What're you gonna use it for...if you don't mind me asking."

Mary rolled her eyes. "Don't act like you're giving me a whole lot of money. It's four hundred dollars. Our rent alone is $740."

With a growing smile, Pedro took a packet of hundreds out of his pocket and began adding to the cash he'd given to Mary at the bar.

"Five...six...seven...eight. There you go. Rent plus sixty extra bucks. For the trouble your friend had in my country." He leaned forward and offered the $800 to Mary.

Reluctantly, she reached out and accepted it. "You should work for me," he said.

"No thanks." Mary put the cash in her bra. "We both have jobs. Full-time jobs. Legal jobs."

"Yeah?"

"Yeah."

"You really should at least consider it. I'd pay triple what you're making now, and I'll even pay off your college debts when you're done." He drank from his glass of champagne and waited for an answer.

Mary eyed him for a long moment, during which time Lisa got up and went to a seat of her own. Lisa's face looked abnormally pale. The blood seemed to have been sucked from underneath her makeup. There was a cut an inch to the side of her left eye that deserved a stitch or three.

"Don't throw up in my car," Pedro said.

"Oh, please." Mary rolled her eyes. "Your cousin is Alexus Costilla. I'm sure you can afford to get this darned thing cleaned."

"Yeah, but still..." He trailed off.

His iPhone 6 rang with a call from Enrique, his cousin Alexus's head of security. He answered and listened. Enrique's men were unloading three submarines somewhere on the California coast. Each submarine contained approximately eight thousand kilos of uncut Colombian cocaine that was purchased from the Medellin Cartel for $1,800 per kilogram.

In the US, each kilo would go for at least ten times that.

36

The Cocaine Princess 8

Ending the call, Pedro was all smiles. His SUV and the two others following it were pulling into the well-lit parking lot at the Good Luck Café.

"Shall we eat in?" Pedro asked.

Lisa nodded her head yes. "I need to go to the restroom...and not by myself."

A chuckle from Pedro. "I'll send two of my men. They're both legally armed. If there's a problem, the shooting will be justified."

"Something tells me you're not wrapped too tight up here." Mary tapped a fingertip on her forehead and pushed open her door.

An old Mexican lady was standing outside the restaurant's entrance as Pedro and the girls got out of the Escalade. She was poorly dressed and obviously homeless, holding a Starbucks cup that was half full of coins. Two Mexican teenagers wearing matching Houston Rockets jerseys were sitting in a customized Mitsubishi a couple of spaces down from where Pedro's SUV was parked, eating burritos and listening a Pit Bull song.

Pedro studied the old lady as he passed her and entered the restaurant. Her gray ASCAP shirt was layered in filth: dirt, food, and whatever else she'd

gotten into since the shirt was last washed, if it ever had been. Her hands were thick and calloused. The underside of her fingernails were caked with dirt.

Pedro went directly to a table at the back wall and picked up a menu while the girls headed for the restroom. He sent four men to make sure the young ladies would not experience another kidnapping attempt this night.

A waitress with the name Penny on her name tag looked in Pedro's direction but he told her to hold fast. His friends were in the restroom. He'd wait for them.

Easing back in his chair, he dug in his pocket for the packet of hundreds he'd used to help out the American girls and peeled off two hundreds. He laid the two bills on the table and put the packet away.

He suddenly found himself envisioning him and Mary alone in his Escalade. He saw himself handing her the entire $10,000 packet of hundreds and then watching her take off the cute little dress while he freed his manhood and sheathed it in a condom. He saw her mounting him, smelled that intense citrus perfume drifting up into his flaring nostrils...

It took him a couple of seconds to shake off the daydream when he noticed that Mary and Lisa were walking toward him.

Some of the color had returned to Lisa's face. She sat across from Pedro, folded her arms on the table, and laid the side of her face down on them.

Mary sat next to her intoxicated friend. "She threw up as soon as we got in there. Drunk ass. I told her not to drink so much."

An erection was bulging in Pedro's slacks. He was glad that they were seated. The waitress came and he ordered Chile Con Carne and the Works burger with fries. He ordered the same meals for his bodyguards. Mary got two double cheeseburgers and two fries for her and Lisa. All of them got Cokes for their beverages.

"I hope they don't take forever with our food. I'm really trying to get this girl home and in bed," Mary said.

"She'll be fine. A little alcohol's never hurt anybody." Pedro glanced at the old lady outside. He slid one of the hundreds he'd laid on the table to Mary. "Wanna do me a favor?"

"Depends on what kind of risk it entails," she replied with a smirk. "Just go out there and give that lady this hundred dollars and my phone

number. Tell her I've got a place for her to stay if she needs one. Here"— he took an ink pen from his shirt pocket, wrote his cell phone number on a

napkin, and placed it atop the Benjamin— "just give this to her. Tell her the sooner she calls the sooner she'll be taken care of."

Mary regarded Pedro with a long questioning stare. He smiled and went to scrolling through his smartphone's text messages. Finally, she got up, and his eyes again studied her slender figure as she walked away.

"Your friend is one sexy piece of chocolate," he mumbled to the sleeping beauty across the table from him. "Makes me wish I'd have stayed in college."

Lisa didn't move. She was completely out of it.

By the time Mary returned a couple of minutes later, the waitress was coming with their plates. Mary's disposition seemed happier all of a sudden. She sat down, beaming.

"Are you trying to get me out of this dress?" Mary asked.

The question caught Pedro off guard. He had no immediate reply. He bit into three French fries and chewed. He'd never been good with women.

Luckily he was rich. His wealth was usually enough to get what he wanted. "That was very kind of you, sir." Mary's voice was warm enough to melt a

snowman. "She hurried away around the side of the building, said she was getting a hotel room for the night and that she'd call you for sure in the morning. That was nice thing you did for her. It was nice what you did for me, too. Thanks. I really appreciate it."

Pedro only nodded and started in on his meal. His entourage were the restaurant's only customers. It was 9:50 pm, ten minutes until closing time. One employee was mopping the floor while another was cleaning tables.

Mary ate in silence until Lisa lifted her head and unleashed a roaring burp that made everyone twist up their faces in disgust.

"Ugh...that was so trife," Mary said, leaning away from her friend.

Lisa said: "He thinks you're a hot piece of chocolate. I heard him mumble it when you left out a minute ago."

An embarrassed chuckle escaped Pedro's throat as he too bobbed away from the horrendous blow of air.

Then his iPhone rang.

This time it was not a text but a call from Enrique.

Enrique only called when something serious needed to be said. Their phones were equipped with government level scrambling devices, but Enrique still had a habit of keeping the calls to a minimum.

"Yes," Pedro answered.

"That group of Zetas who branched off and went with Jenny back in the day, remember them?"

"How could I not?"

"Yeah, well," Enrique said, " they're the same group who were with the guy who sent the suicide bomber at Alexus."

"So what? The guy got his fucking head cut off. They want trouble in Mexico? We'll slaughter them."

"It's not Mexico where they're wanting the trouble. Chicago's the problem.

I just got word that they're gathering for an attack someone in the coming hours." Enrique paused.

Pedro was staring into Mary's pretty brown eyes.

"They have a few hundred kilos that managed to slip through our detection at the border. They've been fronting a lot of it to the Latin Kings in Chicago. Rumor is, the Kings are planning to kill Blake. Tonight."

Blake King was the unofficial boss of the Costilla Cartel until Alexus regained consciousness.

Pedro knew that he couldn't let anything happen to Blake.

Chapter 6

Blake's grin was considerably dim for a man who was watching a trio of gorgeous strippers twerk and swing around the stripper pole Alexus had had installed in front of the large white leather sofa at the foot of the bed.

He had taken $100,000 in hundreds out of his Louis Vuitton duffle bag to make it rain with, and now $30,000 of it was on the white marble floor, being trampled by the six-inch heels under the girls' designer shoes.

The revelation of Tiff's son's paternity had him thinking.

Of course there was the likely chance that Tiff-Tiff was wrong. He remembered her dating another guy— Craig, who he'd shot dead in Miami Beach — so there was that possibility.

He would get a paternity test first thing tomorrow.

Shaken from his reverie by Barbie's bouncing ass as she backed it up onto his lap, Blake momentarily forgot about Tiff-Tiff and the kid.

His dick grew hard almost instantly. He wrapped an arm around her waist and kissed the middle of her back.

"Hope you got some rubbers," Barbie said. She guided his hand to her breast and he squeezed it.

He had more than enough condoms. He had Magnums, the only size that fit his foot-long phallus. He took two of them out of his Balmain jeans and set them down next to him.

Seeing the condoms set the girls in motion. Barbie shoved Blake back on the bed and began unfastening his LV belt. Within seconds she had his jeans and boxers down to his knees and his dick clenched in both hands. Bubbles and Nona climbed up on the bed and started removing his shirt. Bubbles had his shoulder-holster off in no time; she put it on the dresser where another of his guns— a gold-plated .50-Caliber Desert Eagle— was resting between several piles of cash and three diamond necklaces.

Nona attempted to take off the bulletproof vest he had on beneath the shirt but he stopped her.

He'd been shot far too many times in the past to take off his vest while the album release party guests were still leaving the mansion. The camera monitors on the east wall of the bedroom showed the guests as they were walking out the front door.

Barbie sucked the head of his dick into her mouth and then went to work.

She bobbed and licked on its crown while Nona and Bubbles ran their tongues along its sides.

Fatigued from the long day he'd had, Blake laid back and stared up at the 24-karat gold and diamond framed ceiling mirror. He took a deep breath.

The paternity test tried to creep into his mind, along with the threat on his life from the Black Disciples, but he quickly blocked the thoughts out and looked down at the girls as they sucked and licked every inch of his thick love muscle.

Nona and Bubbles went from kissing and licking Blake to kissing and fondling each other. Barbie took the opportunity to deepthroat him while Nona lay next to him and opened her legs for Bubbles to feast.

"Damn," Blake said, overwhelmed by the sight of three beautiful women in his bed.

He sat up, and Barbie put the condom on his saliva-coated phallus. She squeezed and massaged it, looking up at him as her hands jerked rapidly on his pole.

Wasting no time, he moved back on the large bed and inhaled sharply as Barbie mounted him and guided his dick into her lubricious pussy. She
looked amazing with the white diamonds on her neck and wrist. She was a yellowbone, like Nona, only Barbie was smaller with a more perfectly shaped phatty behind her and perkier breasts in front of her. She put the flat of her hands on his thick gold and diamond necklaces and bounced up and down for a long while, moaning and mashing her breasts together, biting her bottom lip and dropping her head back to look at herself in the ceiling mirror.

She turned around moments later and rode him reverse-cowgirl style. He slapped her ass a couple of times. Nona and Bubbles switched to a 69, with Bubbles on top, and Blake stretched an arm out to rub and squeeze Bubbles' ass while Barbie rode him recklessly. Her pussy was warm and tight and creamy-wet. Her moans were the sexiest sounds he'd heard in a long time.

Then his brain hit him with another invasive thought.

He didn't know a single thing about Barbie except that she was the most popular stripper in Atlanta. He knew she made good money, but like most strippers she was more than likely on the prowl for the ultimate come up, like Blac Chyna and Amber Rose. She probably just wanted a wealthy sponsor, a sugar-daddy of sorts, and Blake was a prime candidate.

He decided that later he would Google her. It wasn't smart to be sailing blindly through a relationship, no matter how long he planned for it to last.

She traded places with Bubbles, who was a bit heavier but just as thick where it counted most. She squatted down on his dick and then began slamming her massive ass up and down so roughly that he had to hold on to her waist.

He still had $70,000 stacked up next to him on the bed. He tore off a one of the "$10,000" paper money wraps, tossed the entire ten grand in the air over Barbie, and watched the bills land on her back and all around her on the bed.

A couple of minutes later he put Bubbles on her back, pushed her legs up so that her knees were by her ears, and pounded in and out of her. She moaned. She said she was coming. Then she came and soaked his dick with her juices.

He kept right on pounding, occasionally glancing at his swinging chains and the glistening diamond watch on his wrist. When Bubbles' moans became near-screams he put a packet of hundreds in her mouth for her to bite down on.

He had missed Bubbles just as much as he'd missed Nona, which is why he left Bubbles' legs trembling and then moved over to Nona for yet another knees-by-the-ears fuck.

He was still fucking her when someone knocked at the door. "I'm busy!" Blake shouted immediately.

"It's me, bruh. Biggs."

Nona's eyes became as wide as saucers at the sound of her brother's voice.

Blake paused with his rigid pole buried deep inside Nona.

Barbie kept sucking Bubbles' clit and making the thick brown-skinned woman squirm and moan ecstatically.

"Yup, one minute. Gettin' dressed," Blake said, smiling down at Nona's nervous expression.

Biggs laughed. "A'ight, I'm the dumbest muhfucka alive." Another laugh. "I'm down the hall wit' Young. Hurry up, we boutta hit the streets.

Everybody's slidin' to the club. The Visionary Lounge."

"Yup, Mighty," Blake said, and smiled at the sound of Biggs's footsteps heading down the hall.

He pressed his lips tightly against Nona's and pounded deeply for a few more minutes. Then he tensed up and dug in as deep as he could. His phallus twitched and spilled a copious load in the Magnum.

"You're even handsome...when you come," Nona said breathlessly. She smiled up at him and he gave her a quick peck on the cheek before snatching up his bundles of hundreds and stepping back from the bed with the to pull up his boxers and pants. When he got his belt on he took the cum-filled condom to the bathroom and flushed it.

Then, looking himself in the mirror, he washed his face and cleaned himself off.

The next thing he knew, Barbie was scowling at him from the doorway, and Nona and Bubbles were stepping into the glass-walled shower.

"The fuck you muggin' me for?" he asked Barbie.

"Because I just found out you bought cars for both of these bitches and I'm still fucking carless in Atlanta."

"You ain't been back to Atlanta since we met," Blake countered. "Shit, you can go to Atlanta right now. I'll fly you there and get you a car too...as long as you promise to stay there and not to come back here with that attitude."

She sucked her teeth and snickered as she joined the girls in the shower. For a few minutes Blake put half his attention on their stunning reflections in the sink mirror, watching them shower and chat about the ongoings of Love and Hip Hop Hollywood.

Meanwhile, he Googled "Baddie Barbie", Barbie's stripper name.

There were dozens of links to videos of her dancing onstage at Onyx and Magic City in Atlanta. He went to one of them and watched her shake her ass in front of Lil Wayne and Rick Ross as the two rap titans showered her with dollars. He admired the Versace shirt Ross was wearing and decided he'd go Versace shopping online later tonight. He gawked at Baddie Barbie's beautifully bouncing derrière and almost canceled his search into Barbie's identity.

Then he thought of all the gunshot wounds he'd suffered in the past and pushed on, going through two more pages before running across an NBC news article on Tasia "Baddie Barbie" Olsen's Dade County arrest for felony drug possession on February 14th of last year.

The excited expression he'd worn since the threesome vanished in an instant. It was replaced by a tight face and speculating eyes as he began reading the article.

He had very good reason to be curious now.

He had killed Jantasia Olsen in Mexico, after listening to her make a threatening phone call to an enemy of his asking the guy to kill him. Then he'd killed Jantasia's best friend, a Harlem girl named Ceriniti Stingley. The two were considered as good as dead by Mexican and American authorities, though their bodies were never found.

The article said that Barbie was caught leaving a Red Lobster restaurant with a suspect who had moments earlier sold seventy-two ounces of cocaine to a confidential informant in the parking lot. Upon his arrest, police had found an additional four ounces in Barbie's purse. They'd each been given $100,000 bonds.

He put his phone down and turned to stare at Barbie. Now that he knew who she was possibly related to, he saw the facial similarities Barbie shared with Jantasia.

They could pass for sisters.

"Barbie, lemme talk to you in the bedroom," Blake said, growing more and more furious by the moment.

"Boy, don't you see I'm in here cleaning my—"

"I ain't tryna hear that shit. Come on." Blake snatched open the shower door, reached in the shower, and grabbed a handful of Barbie's hair while pulling his Glock from the holster with his other hand.

Both Barbie and Nona yelped as Blake dragged Barbie out of the shower and threw her up onto the sink. Bubbles gasped and slapped a hand to her mouth. The back of Barbie's head put a big crack in the sink mirror, and before she could fully recover he had the gun's barrel in her mouth.

"The fuck are you doin' here? Huh? Tasia! You thought I wouldn't figure that shit out?!" He gritted his teeth, taking the gun out of her mouth.

"I was only tryna find out who killed my sister!" Tasia sounded frantic.

Blood on the back of her head was reflected in the jagged shards of glass in the mirror. "We don't know what happened to her. I just wanted to —"

"Why are you here? Just answer that?" Tasia only sobbed. She had no answer.

"Get the fuck out my house," Blake said calmly. "The only reason I'm not killing you is because we're in my mansion. If we were anywhere else you'd be dead, too." He went to the intercom in the bedroom and told the butler to send up security to escort little miss Barbie off the premises.

Ten minutes later he was alone in the backseat of his Maybach with his trusty old Louis Vuitton duffle bag full of cash and guns sitting next to him and his two iPhones on his lap. Remo was speeding out of the driveway behind Meach's Wraith and Biggs's Ferrari.

Bubbles sent a text message to Blake asking if the $40,000 he'd thrown in the bedroom was for her and Nona. He told her of course it was.

It certainly wasn't for Barbie. Meach called.

"Straight to The Visionary Lounge?" he asked.

"Yup." Blake nodded. "Hit Cup up and tell him we on our way. Any fuck niggas there we got gunshots for em."

Chapter 7

Chicago, South Side

Englewood had been shooting-free for a couple of hours. In the notoriously violent south side, even a single hour without hearing gunshots was a relief.

That alone was good enough for Porsche Clark to bring out the grill to barbecue and feed the people on her block.

She and her boyfriend, Glo, were sitting on the hood of Porsche's recently Range Rover in the yard behind their house on 64th and Eberhart, watching her 17-year-old neighbor Sasha compete against a girl from further down the street in a twerking contest. The grill was going and stacked high with drumsticks, wings, burgers, and sausages. Three coolers packed full of ice, beers, and sodas sat beneath a table covered with everything they'd need for the night — plates, utensils, eight bottles of Remy Martin, cups, and five big dishes of other foods they would be eating.

Glo had a cup of Lean and a blunt that he was refusing to pass to anyone. He was a high ranking member of the Black Disciples from "O-Block", the Parkway Gardens buildings on 64th and Calumet. The thirty or more young guys and girls gathered in the alleyway and backyard with Porsche and Glo were also affiliated with the BDs, if they weren't actual members already.

A couple of them were doing well for themselves. The few who were in Chief Keef's Glo Gang, or Fredo Santana's Savage Squad Records, or Lil Durk's Only The Family, were doing the most. They had two BMWs, a Panamera, and a Corvette parked in the alleyway, and they had brought their own bottles of Remy, ounces of Kush, and boxes of cigars.

Many others were small-time dealers and stick-up kids, killers and violent felons with itchy trigger fingers and itchy palms. Most of them had dreadlocks. Their cars — if they drove any at all — were for the most part stolen or rented from local drug addicts.

Porsche was glad that she was on their good side. Her being the girlfriend of Glo, one of the BD's most respected members, put her in with the gang. Oftentimes the kilos of coke and heroin she occasionally bought from Mercedes Costilla, her older sister, were broken down to grams and sold by the lower-level dealers. The guys with their own money usually copped weight from Glo, though the product still belonged to Porsche. She was essentially the biggest drug connect in Englewood. She tried not to splurge too much but her Range Rover and Glo's sleek gray Navigator (he'd crashed an Escalade of his during a shootout last week) were the center of attention. Both SUVs sported chrome 30-inch Forgiato rims and glossy candy paint.

The six 12-inch speakers in the rear of Porsche's was currently blasting a Lil Durk song that had all the youngsters turnt up.

"Durk hit my line a lil bit ago," Glo said to Porsche. "He talkin' that peaceful shit Twin Varney n'em on. He don't want us goin' at Bulletface. I said fuck all dat and hung up. Dat nigga gon' pay like he weigh to da folks, on David. I ain't goin' for nothin' else."

"Yeah, make that bitch nigga pay." Porsche nodded her head in agreement. It had been her who'd talked Glo into extorting Blake in the first place. "My medical bills ain't cheap. That bitch Alexus had me shot; now, her husband will pay up if he still wants to do performances in Chicago or he'll be shot too. Simple as that. Shit, I really want the nigga dead. He's lucky to be getting a way out of this shit."

"That's what the fuck I'm sayin'. Nigga better just pay up or get sprayed up. Period."

"Mercedes should be out of the hospital in the next week or so. She's coming here to stay with us until she heals up from that damn suicide bombing. Her ass shouldn't't've been hanging around Alexus in the first damn place. We know she's one of those Mexican cartel bitches. It's too dangerous bein' around that hoe."

"That bitch ain't seen dangerous," Glo said, and took two tremendous gulps of Lean. He was a hulk of a man with bulging muscles, a beer belly, and tattoos from face to abdomen. His shirt was off. His True Religion jeans were cinched to his waist by a Gucci belt.

Porsche's eyes remained glued to Sasha's jaw-dropping dance moves.

Sasha was a 17-year-old with a 27-year-old's curves. Now one of Porsche's closest friends, the teen had the kind of Coke bottle figure that made men stop and stare wherever she went. Aside from Porsche's older sister, Sasha was the baddest bitch she'd ever actually hung out with on a consistent basis. Sasha was the realest friend, always texting and calling and Facetiming when they weren't together, always wanting to stay when they were.

Which explained why Porsche had spent almost $20,000 on gifts— mostly shoes, bags, and clothes — for Sasha's 17th birthday party two days prior. After all her years of misfortune with friends and lovers on the city's west side, she now had a man and a friend who both loved her unconditionally. All it had taken was her moving to the most dangerous neighborhood in Chicago.

"I'm thinking about getting Sash a car," she said, more to herself than to Glo. "Nothing too crazy. Maybe like a 2015 Impala, you know. Something
she can show out in."

"That or get me somethin'. Ya know." Glo laughed. "Nah, but seriously, she's a cool lil chick. Knew her since she was a shorty."

Glo seemed to be getting ready to say more but Sasha was walking to them so he shut up.

She was out of breath. Beads of sweat lined her forehead.

Porsche said: "Bitch, don't bring yo lil musty ass over here now. Go on and finish dancing." She made a face that feigned disgust. Sasha flipped up a middle finger, and both of them cracked up laughing.

"Did you see me just put it on that lil thot from down the street?" Sasha said. She took a second to pour a cold bottle of water over her face and then continued. "But fuck her, it's what her brother just said that got me on one. The nigga claim his big cousin Milly n'em at the The Visionary Lounge out west right now wit' Bulletface, Biggs, and Meach. He say they took over the VIP section, got everybody in there poppin' bottles."

Sasha looked from Porsche to Glo and back to Porsche again. She wore a red Prada jumpsuit with absolutely nothing on underneath it and black and red Jordan sneakers. She and Porsche were matching, only Porsche's jumpsuit was a few shades lighter and Porsche's purse was a sixteen- thousand-dollar Hermes Birkin while Sasha's was an eighteen-hundred- dollar Prada. Still, the bags were red, and the girls were the shit compared to all the other girls.

Glo hopped down from the Range Rover's hood and shouted

for everyone to get ready to roll out.

"What about all this barbecue?" Porsche asked. "Give these lil niggas some food to—"

"Fuck all dat shit. We gon' fuck around and make Bulletface pay enough to make us all rich tonight. We finna slide on that nigga ten cars deep. All da girls stay here."

Slowly, a conspiratorial smile crept across Porsche's dark-hued face. The expression grew steadily as she watched Glo reach in the bushes next to their back stairs and lift out an AR-15 with a 100-round dual drum magazine.

"I'll be back, baby. On David, don't be out here fuckin' wit' these lil niggas. Stay the fuck in the house. Shit boutta get hectic."

"I know, baby. Be safe." She leapt into his arms and gave him a kiss. Then he set her on the grass and climbed in his Navigator.

Every one of the gang's whips drove swiftly out of the alley and toward their destination.

"Think they gon' kill Bulletface?" Sasha asked Porsche.

"I wouldn't be sad if they did," was Porsche's honest reply.

Chapter 8

Slide up wit' dat K on me when it's summer time cause it's drill season Facebook and Twitter beefin', that'll get you wacked for no real reason Fuck a hatin ass nigga, long as I'm still breathin we still eatin'

If they start bluffin' I'm gon' start bussin', check the news to see if they still breathin'

Every nigga in my hood know...I keep poles on me like stop signs

And when it's drama I slide through, roll the window down and it's shots fired

Shoot till my fingers got tired, for a thot bitch I ain't got time

My right hand on the Holy Bible, I'm the truth nigga I am not lyin'

I been gang for a long time, used to ride around with that chrome nine Sellin' hard white all day and night, 24/7 that's a long grind

Made it big... we on now, got the whole town wit they palms out

Ion break bread wit no fuck nigga, fuck what all you niggas be talm bout Got a problem wit it, thirty shots'll fix it...'

"Drill Season"— Biggs's song featuring Bulletface — had already been blasting when the MBM gang made it inside The Visionary Lounge's VIP section; now it was playing for the third time in less than an hour. Most of the celebs and strippers who'd attended the album release party were also in VIP. Blake had purchased 500 bottles of Ace of Spades, including ten large $20,000 bottles for himself, his MBM artists, and a few others rappers.

He had two boxes full of one-dollar bills, $250,000 in total, stacked on his table. He and Meach were throwing fistfuls of dollars over the balcony at the strippers on the stage below; Cup had given Maliah, one of Blake's favorite dancers, $10,000 to fly in from Houston for tonight's event, and she was killing the pole, taking most of the attention from the other two strippers that were onstage with her. Waitresses were traversing the crowded floor down there, handing out the expensive bottles of champagne Blake had purchased to the best dressed men and women in the building.

Texas rappers Chedda Da Connect and Bun B were in the building, posted up two tables down from Blake's. Yo Gotti and his CMG squad were next to them. Soon they all would be performing a few of their hit records for the crowd of over 2,500 club-goers.

Cup, the club owner, was the high yellow businessman in a crisp black suit and gold tie who was standing next to Blake, smiling his charming smile at every camera flash. He was a man Blake had known for years, a high-ranking Traveling Vice Lord from Chicago's Lawndale neighborhood who'd raised Lil Lord— Blake's mentor and longtime friend— and eventually became one of Blake's best drug-pushers, getting rid of hundreds upon hundreds of cocaine bricks every month.

There was always a thinly veiled tension between the two bosses.

Cup had been behind the kidnapping of Blake's daughter and the murder of his daughter's mother several years prior. If not for a piece of advice Alexus's father had given Blake regarding the separation of personal and business relations in the drug game, he knew that either he or Cup would be dead by now.

Blake's eyes were glued Maliah.

"Be careful what you wish for," Cup said, giving Blake a nudge with an elbow. "Tahiry is on her way. You know she wants to rekindle that flame she sparked in New York. Plus, I know you got Barbie ducked off somewhere. Don't do too much."

That's when it struck Blake.

It had been Cup who'd practically sat Barbie in Blake's lap.

"I don't know where dat bitch Barbie at," Blake said, suddenly more into studying Cup than ogling Maliah. "You should know better than me. You put the bitch on me."

"Between me and you, she promised to give me some pussy if I plugged her witchoo. I figured we could both fuck her and charge it to the game."

"That's Jantasia's sister, nigga," Blake said, a bit more bitterly than he'd intended. "She was on settin' me up. Her family think I had somethin' to do with Jantasia gettin' murked."

Cup seemed genuinely surprised. "Damn, for real?"

"Nah, for play," Blake said sarcastically. He went to his table and sat down. There were already a dozen blunts in rotation. He grabbed one from Biggs and filled his lungs. Cup stood next to the table.

"You're a smart man," Cup said. "I'm sure she wouldn't have been able to set you up even if she wanted to."

"You hear anything about some niggas putting some money on my head?" Blake paid close attention to Cup's facial movements in hopes of catching the slick businessman in a lie.

"Yeah." Cup nodded. "I think they want some money from you for that little trouble you caused young Sosa. Ask Durk about that. Think it's some niggas from out his way."

Blake shook his head no and gritted his teeth. The anger compelled him to take in another chest full of smoke and mouthful of Lean. He wasn't about to ask anyone about a thing. He was the fucking king of the world. He was Bulletface. He was Blake King. He was the wealthiest real street nigga in American history.

His emotions must have shown on his face.

Biggs, sitting to the right of Blake, leaned over to him and said, "Don't let pride get in the way, bruh. It might be smart to put them niggas on the team. Give em a lil somethin' to trap wit' if that's what they want. I'll give it to em if you don't want to. Like Abraham Lincoln said, you destroy your enemies when you join forces wit em."

"Man, I know you didn't just try to quote Abraham Lincoln." Blake laughed and shook his head.

Perhaps Biggs was right, though. It certainly wouldn't hurt Blake's pockets to give a little. Maybe by giving he'd learn who'd made the call to extort him in the first place.

The drank and Kush had Blake in a daze. Soon he returned to the balcony and finished watching Maliah dance while people on the crowded first floor level aimed their smartphones at him, snapping pictures and recording video. Then he watched Chedda Da Connect perform "Flicka Da Wrist" and raised his own wrist to show off his white diamond Hublot watch.

Just as Yo Gotti's "Errrbody" began booming from the club's many overhead speakers, and as the king of Memphis himself was taking the stage, Blake spotted Tahiry making her way through the crowd.

He grinned and then chuckled. A quick glance to his right revealed that Maliah was just entering the VIP section.

Her eyes were glued to him. She gave the other celebrities hugs and started toward Blake. He remembered her and a few other strippers dancing for him at his bachelor's party. Someone had ruined the night shortly after

the party had started, but the memory of Maliah's phat ass on his lap was unforgettable.

But damn, now Tahiry was here. He didn't know which dime piece was the better option, or if either of them would be content with dealing with hook at all.

Maliah made it to Blake and planted her hands on her hips. "Hey, black ass boy." Her warm smile was warm and addictive. She'd changed into a white minidress. She spun around to give him a full panoramic view of her curves.

"Damn," Blake said. "Look like you done got thicker." He gave her a soft hug.

"I've been trying to reach you for the longest." She smiled and inched closer, so that their pelvises were connected. "Bulletface. Sexy man. Are we going to finish what we started that night?"

"That's up to you."

"If it's up to me then we should be leaving right now." "I just got here."

"You don't wanna stay, either." She looked around the room, then added: "I overheard some niggas downstairs saying something was about to go down. Somebody's on the way here to start trouble. I think it's some of Durk's people."

Chapter 9

Glo blew through the stoplight at the intersection of Chicago Avenue and Laramie and veered into The Visionary Lounge's vast parking lot. He almost hit a heavyset girl as he pulled into one of only three available parking spots. She cursed him until her friend snatched her away.

"Fat ass bitch better go sit down somewhere," Glo said, lighting a cigarette. He hardly gave the fat bitch a glance. He had Caper, one of the few BD's that was his age, sitting next to him.

Slender, light-complected, and thuggishly-comported in a True Religion outfit, Caper was an OG who'd just gotten out of prison to a blessing of

$20,000 from the mob. He had a black steel .45 caliber pistol with an extended clip on his lap and a Styrofoam of Lean in hand.

Lil Durk's Remember My Name album was booming from the large speakers in the rear of the SUV.

"Folks, we ain't gotta wack this nigga," Caper said, rolling his window down as Lamron Twin pulled his gray Camaro on big chrome rims into the parking space next to him. "We can really just connect with the nigga and get way more. Shit, he got over a billion! You think he won't let us eat with him? You should've came at the nigga wit' respect instead of just demandin' some shit. Who gave you the idea any-muhfuckin-way? And don't say that lil thottie you live wit'."

Glo shook his head and chuckled. A smirk grew.

"I knew it," Caper said in triumph. "Fuck what that bitch on. She probably just don't like that nigga 'cause she got shot in Barbados after they released pictures of that sextape of her and Bulletface. We can get money and win with this nigga. You see him and Sosa squashed that shit. We gotta do the same. And like I say, he's a billionaire. On David. A real life muhfuckin billionaire. You don't meet niggas like him every day. We can play the cool role and get way more out of this nigga than we could if we extorted him."

"That nigga got too much money for the streets not to be eatin' off him," Glo reasoned. "Especially wit' all this Chiraq shit the nigga keep talkin' in his raps. He ain't even from out here."

"His guy Lil Lord is. Lord damn near raised the lil nigga. One of the Travs off 15th and Trumbull. That's why Bulletface and Cup so tight; you know Cup the king out there, like the next Neal Wallace."

Glo could only nod and sip his drink. He'd been duped into wanting to extort Bulletface by a woman he hardly even knew, a woman with her own personal issues between herself and the rap star.

Caper told Twin and the other gang members to hold off on any aggression, but he and Glo still put the guns on their hips as they climbed out of the SUV.

Fourteen deep, the gang gathered in front of their vehicles, passing around blunts and sipping Lean, glancing around at the passing traffic on Chicago Avenue.

Caper and Twin discussed a beef with some BrickSquad GD's. The "bricks" (a derogatory term for the Gangster Disciples) had allegedly gunned down one of the guys in an alleyway yesterday, and Twin wanted payback.

Glo listened in complete silence. He was thinking of a new plan; suddenly plan A didn't seem so wise.

He contemplated calling Porsche and getting on her for being so manipulative. What if he'd ended up dead or with a life sentence over this whole extortion idea.

He gave in to the fact that it was ultimately his fault for falling victim to her conniving words. He was from the slums where having game was imperative, yet he'd let a skinny little thot from out west drag him into a beef with the king of rap.

A heavy thud came from the rear of the club.

Glo looked toward the sound just in time to see Lil Durk and his OTF affiliates emerging from the nightclub's rear exit ahead of Bulletface and his MBM artists. Behind the MBM group were four of the baddest women Glo had ever laid eyes on.

Chapter 10

It all happened in an instant.

When Blake saw the circle of gangsters standing across the parking lot, he instinctively dropped his Styrofoam cups and the blunt he had in his left hand and slipped a hand in his duffle bag. He wrapped his fingers around the handle of his Mac-11.

Maliah and Tahiry gasped in unison and stepped back into the club with the other two women.

"Gang," Durk said loudly, "we ain't on that. We gettin' money. Fuck all dat bullshit."

The latest man at the front of the group said: "We good, on folks n'em—"

The man was still speaking when an older model Cutlass pulled up to the parking lot's entrance.

Meach elbowed Blake and murmured: "Look, bruh" just as the barrel of an assault rifle was pushed out of the Cutlass's passenger window.

At the same moment, a black Escalade came screeching to a half on the other side of the Cutlass.

Gunfire began lighting up the night.

Blake ducked beside a Chevy pickup just as bullets started pinging through its other side.

He knew then that the bullets were meant for him. But the gunfire stopped as suddenly as it had begun.

The black Escalade sped off, and Blake raised up to open fire on the Cutlass.

Meach and Biggs drew Glocks from their waists and sent a dozen shots at the Cutlass, while the gang of men Blake had considered a threat seconds prior shot up the escaping Escalade. Blake sprayed bullets into the Cutlass's passenger door. Durk and a few of his hitters joined in on the Swiss- cheesing of the Oldsmobile.

The big guy Durk had shouted to ran up to the bullet-riddled car and sent four more shots into the passenger window, while Blake rushed to the rear passenger side door of his Maybach and yanked it open.

Remo, his driver, was ducked down in the driver's seat.

"Drive, nigga!" Blake shouted as he slammed his door shut.

"The fuck I pay you for?"

"Not for this shit. That's for damn sure." Remo's graying hair became visible as he slowly raised his head and started the engine. "Whoever wad in that Escalade was on your side, Blake. They started shooting that car up with you."

Blake kept the submachine gun in his hand as Remo gunned the engine and screeched around Meach's Rolls-Royce.

The MBM gang and Durk's OTF crew raced out of the parking lot, followed by the men who'd been waiting behind the nightclub.

They split up, with Blake sticking with his recording artists and Durk speeding off in the opposite direction with his gang.

Blake decided it was time to fly out to Los Angeles. He had a feeling that if he stayed a moment longer in Chicago, his reign as the king of rap might suddenly come to an end.

Chapter 11

"WHY WOULD YOU DO SOMETHING LIKE THAT?!" Mary screamed at the top of her lungs. "There are literally bullet holes stitched all across the side of this truck. Why would you pull up and get involved in a fucking shootout!"

Pedro didn't understand why Mary seemed so distressed; the Escalade was armored. No harm could come to either of them. He had to admit, the bullets stuck in the windows were disturbing, but there was no need to be getting all upset about it.

"Settle down," he said, holding on to the soft leather armrests as his driver veered onto a dark side street.

Pedro had convinced the girls into flying with him from El Paso to Chicago, where he'd had an armored SUV identical to the one they'd traveled in from Juarez to El Paso waiting. Mary had at first declined to travel along with him but the remaining $9,000 from his packet of hundreds had done the trick.

The girls hadn't known that Pedro was only stopping in Chicago to guarantee Blake's safety from the Hispanic gangsters that were after him.

From Alexus's bedside way out in Los Angeles, California, Enrique had somehow figured out the location of the gunmen who were going to carry out the hit on Blake. By the time Pedro caught up with the gunmen, they were already pulling up on Blake at The Visionary Lounge.

He'd emptied a miniature AK-47 into the Cutlass just as its passenger began firing at Blake. His assault rifle had quickly put an end to the rookie attack, but then the men in the nightclub's parking lot had sent a barrage of gunshots at him as his driver escaped down Laramie.

Now Mary and Lisa were sitting wide-eyed in their seats across from him, holding on to the armrests like he was, heads lowered in fear of more gunfire.

There was smoke curling up from the barrel of the mini AK-47 on Pedro's lap. When his driver slowed the Escalade, he picked up a white leather briefcase from beside his chair and snapped it open.

Inside the briefcase were two neat rows of hundred-dollar bills in $10,000 bank packets. $250,000 altogether.

He tossed a packet to Mary. "That's for the trouble. Sorry about that. They were after Blake."

The cash landed on Mary's succulent brown thighs. She looked at Pedro.

Her eyes became stringent slits.

Lisa was a bit more competent than she'd been before the flight. Two and a half hours of sleep had sobered her.

"I've come to the conclusion that this fucker is not the brightest crayon in the box," she said. "We agreed to come with the assumption that this would

be a nice little trip, not to star on some kinda America's Most Wanted show."

"I didn't have a choice. They were after Blake," Pedro repeated as he set the briefcase back down. "I don't see the need for complaint. You just got an extra ten grand."

"Get us to a hotel. Now," Mary demanded.

Pedro chuckled and ordered his driver to head back to O'Hare airport. He knew Blake would be on his way there sooner or later.

"I said a hotel," Mary snapped.

"That wasn't part of the deal. Twenty-four hours with me was the deal. My schedule. My plans. Not yours, not Lisa's. Mine. Comprende?"

Mary rolled her eyes. Her upper lip curled in disdain. She fanned through the stack of hundreds and turned to look out her window.

"You'd better not get us arrested," Lisa said, gazing at the camera monitors next to her door. They offered an HD night-vision view from all eight of the Escalade's exterior cameras. A Google Earth view of their location showed on the tablet beneath the camera monitors.

"We're fine," Pedro said. "We have an oceanfront mansion in Malibu, California to visit. Cost me $41 million. We can rest there. I'll take you both shopping first thing tomorrow, maybe introduce you to some of your favorite Hollywood actors. You'll forget all about what's happened tonight."

The two young women didn't respond for a long while. Mary counted through the pile of hundreds and gave half to Lisa, who recounted it as if she suspected Mary was a thief and then quickly stuffed it in her purse and got to work on her smartphone.

Minutes later, Mary said: "Are you all really cartel bosses? It's what they said on ABC news. Saw it the other week."

"They exaggerate," Pedro said. "What do you expect from the news? Truth?" He touched a button that opened the sunroof and took a Cuban cigar from his breast pocket. "Alexus inherited $50 billion from my grandmother. She's half-Mexican, like me. Of course some of that money will be in Mexico. They tie it to the cartels to make us look bad, but we're honestly just a family business. I own a lot of property, you know. Here in the States and also in Mexico. I've built seven schools in my country, all with the billions my family has made off your country. In the stock market, of course. Nothing illegal. Grand, isn't it?" He chuckled heartily.

Mary rolled her eyes again. "Bullshit."

"It's no bullshit. I'm really a good guy. They indicted us because my father was sick in the head. He lied on us, twisted some truths, tried to take over the family business."

"And what exactly is the family business?" Mary inquired. She wore an expression of disbelief.

Pedro thoughtfully lit his cigar. His eyes flicked from Lisa to Mary, from Mary to Lisa, and back to Mary again.

Instead of replying to the invasive question, he grabbed his iPhone and dialed Blake's number.

"No answer?" Mary was persistent. So was Pedro.

He ignored her and put the smartphone to his ear.

King Rio

Chapter 12

A thump in the night awakened Rita Mae Bishop from a sleep that had been peacefully coexisting with the Anita Baker album playing from the Beats speakers on her Honduran mahogany bedside table.

She was lying on her side with her back to the bedroom door, comfortably attired in a black lace Victoria's Secret bra and panties set and a silk Versace scarf to keep her hair in check. King Neal Costilla, her grandson, was asleep next to her, his arms spread out as if he were nailed to an imaginary cross.

Rita sat up and instinctively pushed one of King's arms down to his side; she remembered being nailed to a real cross by her ex-husband's sister, and seeing her grandson in the same pose was troubling.

After stepping into her black fur slippers and a matching robe, Rita went to the bedroom door and opened it a crack.

"Vari?" she called sleepily into the darkness of the hallway.

Vari was Savaria Chanel King, Rita's son-in-law Blake's daughter from the relationship he'd had before meeting Alexus. Vari was rough around the edges like her father but sweet nonetheless. The three of them — Rita, King, and Vari— had been staying at the forty-million-dollar Hollywood mansion ever since Alexus was flown here to California for surgery following the Indianapolis hotel blast.

Stepping out into the hallway, Rita again called for Vari, and again she got no reply.

"Lord, if this girl is up this time of night doin' somethin' she ain't got no business..." Rita said as she continued up the long hallway.

When she made it to Savaria's bedroom and peeked in, the little girl was in bed, back to the door like Rita had slept, a Teddy Bear held tight against her chest.

Rita's eyebrows came close together.

Then she heard Vari's tiny giggle and flicked on the light.

"You playin' with me this time of night?" Rita's hands went to her hips.

She squinted against the light.

Vari sat up energetically; she'd obviously already been awake. Clad in a pink and black pajama set Gucci had custom designed for her, the cute little 9-year-old hopped down from her bed and mimicked her grandmother-in- law's stance.

"Lil girl, do you have any idea what time it is? Why are you in here banging around when you're supposed to be asleep?"

Vari cast a glimpse at the glowing red numbers on her bedside clock: 3:05 AM.

"It's 6:05 at our Miami houses," Vari said with a beaming smile. She waved Rita off and scrambled by. "Come on, Grandma, I wanna show you somethin'. In the kitchen. And you gotta promise not to beat me."

"Promises are meant to be broken," Rita muttered as she reluctantly trailed Blake's daughter down the stairs to their kitchen, where a chocolate cake was smashed on its top in the middle of the floor.

"I should —" Rita started. "You promised!"

"Damn that promise, Vari. It's three in the morning, and you're down here trying to eat some cake."

"If my daddy was here he would let me get some cake."

Rita shook her head at the smart-mouthed little girl and leaned her shoulder on the wall. For a couple of seconds she studied the cake, and Vari's innocently guilty brown face. Anita Baker's sweet, soulful voice could still be heard drifting down from upstairs.

There were ten full-time staff members in the mansion. Oddly, neither of them were present. They must have known that a little rascal was running amuck.

"I should wring your neck, Vari. I really should." Rita turned and started walking. She still wasn't used to the new mansion's many rooms and oftentimes she found herself wandering aimlessly. This was one of those times.

When she made it to the family room, she took a seat in an easy chair and switched on the lamp beside it. In the table's only drawer was a Bible that Rita kept there for the sleepless nights when she sat under the lamplight and studied God's word.

The little rascal ended up right next to her.

"Ugh." Vari rolled her eyes. "I am not trying to hear about God again." "God is everything." Rita picked up the Bible. "God is the reason you're so blessed today. He's the reason you have

clothes on your back and a roof
over your head, the reason your future is in your hands."

Vari put her elbows on the arm of the easy chair and rested her chin in her palms. She had rich caramel skin. Her hair was thick and well-groomed.

Her fingernails were perfectly manicured. Her eyes were aglow with the innocence of childhood, though most times her behavior proved to be anything but innocent.

"I got a question, Grandma. Ooh, and it's a good one." "Ask away."

"You remember seeing those commercials about all the hungry kids in Africa?"

Rita nodded and began flipping through pages in the Bible, looking for a good verse to share with Vari.

"Why does God let them starve like that? I mean, they be all skinny and hungry. God ain't blessing them."

"They're alive," Rita answered. "Isn't that enough?"

Vari shook her head. "Nope. I'd rather be dead than be all skinny and hungry. Ooh, and they be broke, too. All homeless and stuff. No clothes. God shouldn't do them like that, Grandma. He should be good to all the people. Why can't they eat good food like us?"

"What's in God's plans is sometimes hard to understand." "Have you ever talked to God?"

"Yes, I have."

"Did He talk back?" "Yes, he did."

Vari drew her right cheek back skeptically. "Nuh uhhhh."

"He spoke back with actions." "You're reaching, Grandma."

A burst of laughter blew from Rita's throat. She planted a hand in Vari's hair and shook the little girl's head.

"Believe in the word of God, baby. No matter what. He's the only one who's always got your back. Don't you ever forget that."

"Mm hmm." Vari's cheek was pulled back again. She walked over to the coffee table, got the television remote, and turned it on.

"I cannot believe you have me woke this time of night," Rita said, steadily flipping through pages.

Vari stopped on TMZ when she heard her father's rap name being mentioned by Charles.

'...Bulletface's rumored relationship with popular stripper

King Rio

Lakita "Bubbles" Thomas is reportedly heating up again while his wife, Alexus Costilla, lies hospitalized in a coma in LA, facing over four hundred federal indictments in connection to the Mexican drug cartel bust that imprisoned several of her family members and many of their close associates...'

"Grandma, is Bubbles my daddy's new girlfriend for real?" "I don't know, baby. Ask your daddy."

"I rather he stay with Lexi." "Me, too."

"My daddy is dumb sometimes." "What man isn't?"

"I wouldn't say it to his face." "Of course you wouldn't."

"Not getting my butt whooped." "We wouldn't want that."

Vari crossed her arms over her chest and went back to surfing the cable channels.

"Deuteronomy 15:11," Rita said. " 'For there will never cease to be poor in the land. Therefore I command you, 'You shall open wide your hand to your brother, to the needy and to the poor, in your land.' That's a great answer to your question, isn't it?"

Vari shrugged and kept her eyes on the TV. "I suppose." She took a deep breath. "Grandma, there's this girl at school who keeps calling me ghetto because I'm black and wasn't raised like she was. Her daddy is a famous movie star or something. He goes to the science church."

A worried frown painted Rita's face. Savaria went to Wilshire, a private school that many Hollywood celebs used to discreetly further their children's education away from the public's eye. It was expensive but well worth every dollar spent. Both King and Savaria now attended the school.

"The science church?" Rita said. "You mean the Church of Scientology?" "I don't know about all that, Grandma. Dang."

"Watch your mouth, little girl," Rita chastised. "And as for the kid who called you ghetto, pay her no mind. Her parents are probably just as foolish. You just focus on keeping up those grades. If you can ever remember some of this good scripture I'm always reading to you share it with your classmates. It'll do all of you some good."

"I don't need no scripture for her. What I need to do is kick her butt, Grandma. Real good. Just one good punch to her eye and she'll never bother me again." Vari sat down on the sofa and crossed her legs Indian-style.

"If you put your hands on her," Rita threatened, "she won't be the only one getting their tail whipped."

"I wouldn't mind my whooping if she got a whooping, too." Vari was all smiles.

Blake's daughter was a trip.

Flipping through the Bible, Rita thought of her own daughter. Alexus's wounds were healing, according to her doctor. There would be stitches and staples and burns but at least Alexus was alive and well. That's all that really mattered to Rita at the end of the day. As long as Alexus was okay, Rita could rest well at night... unless some little rascal with a sweet tooth ruined her sleep over chocolate cake.

"Grandma," Vari said, "I think I understand grownups now." "Oh yeah?"

Vari nodded her head. "Yup. I got it all figured out. Just like us kids be having imaginary friends, y'all grownups got em too. God is your imaginary friend."

"You need Jesus, little girl," Rita concluded. "God is real." "That cake would've been real...real good."

"You need more than Jesus."

"What I need is my daddy. When is he coming to get me and my brother?" "That's a question you'll have to ask your daddy. You can call him in the

morning." Rita stood up, yawning. "I'm going back to bed." "Can I sleep down here?"

"I don't care where you sleep. As long as you don't wake me up." "Love you, Grandma."

"I'm sure you do," Rita said as she left the 9-year-old sitting in the family room and headed back up to bed.

King Rio

Chapter 13

When Blake awoke the following morning he was in bed at the Highland Park mansion, sandwiched between Nona and Bubbles.

For a long while he gazed up at the ceiling with his fingers interlaced behind his head, thinking over all that had transpired last night and wishing he'd stuck around to catch up with Tahiry and Maliah. The women in bed with him were just as stunning but he'd been wanting a night with T&M forever and a day.

Every time he got the chance with either of them, something went wrong.

It never failed.

He thought back to the phone call he'd received from Pedro after the shooting at The Visionary Lounge. A part of him couldn't believe — or perhaps didn't want to believe — that the cartel boss had gone out on a limb to save him from being killed. At first Blake had suspected the Black Disciples of being behind the shooting, but a brief moment of contemplation had put an end to that suspicion. Durk's guys and Blake's team had been on the same side during the shooting. There was no disputing that. Plus, a couple of Blake's dealers were going to drop off two kilos of cocaine to Durk's guys early this morning. From now on, the BD's would be buying their coke from Blake for $16,000-a-ki.

In a single drug deal, he'd eradicated his beef with the Englewood gang and turned it into a profit.

He got up to take a piss and brush his teeth and returned some phone calls while he was at it. His daughter, Vari, had called for nothing other than to say she missed him and that she'd dropped a chocolate cake on the floor last night. His son, King, had a cold and wasn't feeling too good. Rita was alright. Alexus was doing better. Blake promised to be there in LA in a couple of hours and hung up to call his older brother, Terrence "Streets" King, who was always busy managing the MBM record label from his office in Times Square.

Streets informed Blake that Lil Boosie needed the verse Blake had promised for his Touchdown 2 Cause Hell album; it had slipped Blake's mind but he'd already recorded it and in a matter of seconds the verse was emailed to Boosie.

Meach, Biggs, and Will Scrill were scheduled to perform with Bulletface at the Staples Center in Los Angeles at 9:00 pm tonight. Mocha, MBM's princess of R&B, had appearances on two Florida radio shows and a solo concert in Jacksonville at eight. All of MBM's artists were booked throughout the week.

If all went well, Money Bagz Management would make $18.9 million in the coming thirty days.

$12.2 million would go directly to Blake, the CEO of MBM.

The rest of the wealth would be used to pay the remaining artists, handle their traveling expenses, and pay all the necessary people that were hired to pull off every event as flawlessly as humanly possible. This included choreographers, road managers, engineers and music crews, film crews, and security, among other professions.

Blake could almost see his big brother cringe through the phone when he told Terrence about last night's shooting.

"I'm done telling you what I think about that shit, lil bruh. I see you wanna learn the hard way, so do you. You're a grown man," Streets said.

"You ain't gotta tell me shit, nigga. I got me." "You my lil brotha...nigga."

"Well," Blake persisted, turning on the shower and adjusting the water to a comfortable temperature, "you ain't gotta worry about lil bruh. Lil bruh good. I'm a street nigga runnin' shit in Mexico right now. You think I can't handle myself?"

"A'ight, King Blake." Terrence's voice was heavily laced with sarcasm. "I am the king, nigga. Laugh if you wanna but you know the truth. You

just spoke it." Blake grinned, eyeing his reflection in the shards of glass that were left in the corners of his sink mirror and reminiscing about how good the girls in his bed had treated him upon his return home last night. "Listen, bruh. Let me do this shit, a'ight? Let a king be a king. I ain't gon' let myself down."

"Whatever you say, boss."

"You talk to Uncle Noble?" Blake asked.

Noble King, their deceased father's brother, was a porn producer in LA. He'd gotten his foot in the adult entertainment industry with some money Blake gave him and hadn't looked back since.

"Nope," Streets said. "Ain't heard from him. You'll probably hear from him before the concert tonight. You know he gon' show up on some VIP- type shit. Tell his old ass I said call me. And make sure you get to that stadium on time. That's $2 million on the line."

"Yup, I'll hit you when I touch down." Blake ended the call and took a steaming hot ten-minute shower.

The situation with Baddie Barbie weighed heavily on his mind.

He thought maybe he'd went a little too hard on her, throwing her into the mirror like he had. It wasn't like she knew that it was him who'd killed her sister in Mexico. She had come around fishing, trying to find out but never really knowing the truth.

Essentially, he'd told on himself by reacting so harshly to the revelation of her identity.

As he got out of the shower and dried off, he decided it was best to make amends for his assault on the beautiful young stripper. She hadn't deserved to be treated in such a disrespectful way. He thought of his mother, who'd been killed with his father by the Costilla Cartel— the very same drug cartel that he now presided over. Blake's heart ached every time his mom flashed through his mind, and he imagined losing a sister elicited a similar pain.

While Nona and Bubbles showered, and while Blake was putting on a fresh all-white Versace outfit, he set his smartphones on the sink and used one of them to dial Barbie's number.

An angry woman's voice that wasn't Barbie's answered.

"Don't ever in your fucking life call this phone again," she said and hung up immediately.

Blake called back.

"Nigga, you think I'm playin' or somethin'? I said don't call this motha—" "I heard what the fuck you said! Now put Barbie on the muhfuckin phone,

I ain't tryna hear that bullshit."

There was a long pause. The wait didn't bother Blake at all. He calmly dropped a thick gold and white diamond chain with an oversized, diamond- encrusted gold Jesus piece around his neck and started spraying on some cologne.

It was Barbie who replied this time.

"Why are you calling me?" She sounded like she was in tears.

71

The hurt in her voice caught Blake off guard. At first he could think of nothing to say. He stood there frozen at the broken mirror (the glass that had littered the sink and floor when he left last night had been cleaned up, but no one had thought to do anything with the actual mirror) with his bottle of cologne in hand, unsure of himself. He had done wrong to a beautiful Black woman and knowing it hurt his heart to the core and stunned him into silence.

When he finally spoke, he stuttered: "I, uh...I'm sorry, Barbie. That's all I can say. I'm really, really sorry. I honestly didn't mean to do that shit."

"Who killed Jantasia?" she asked sobbingly.

"I have not the slightest idea. For real. She left with Tee-Tee and I never saw her again."

"That's BS." Barbie sniffled. "Tell me the truth, Bulletface. Just tell me the truth."

"I am telling you the truth. She left out going shopping with Cereniti and disappeared. It happens down there in Mexico all the time. The cartels kidnap muhfuckas. I ain't have shit to do with that."

She sniffled again. "I'm suing you for that shit you did last night."

"We can settle that out of court right now. How much it's gon' cost me?

Huh? I'll pay you today. As a matter of fact, where are you? I'll send you the money now."

"I hate you, Bulletface." "Where you at?"

"I am so serious. I hate you so fucking much. I hope you know I got seven staples in the back of my damn head. I am going to sue the black off your ass."

Suddenly Blake was a bit more at ease. He was talking to Barbie; this was a start to righting the wrong he'd done.

"You ain't gotta sue me to get some money. Just tell me where you at and I gotchoo."

She paused again.

Blake entered his huge walk-in closet and selected a couple more heavy gold and diamond jewelry pieces— a Rolex watch, and a custom bracelet and two pinky rings he'd gotten from Jacob the Jeweler.

"I hate you," Barbie repeated, speaking more softly this time. Blake could tell that it was hurt speaking for her.

"I know," he said. "You got the right to hate me. That's what the fuck I get for drinkin' and smokin' all muhfuckin day. I'm done fuckin' around with that syrup."

He grabbed his duffle bag and a white pair of Louboutin sneakers and went to his bed to sit down and go over his social media accounts.

"I'm at my friend's house on the west side," Barbie admitted finally. "My girl Jessica let me stay here after I left the hospital. I didn't wanna go back to the A with a busted head. My sister would kill me."

"You okay?" It was the only thing Blake could think of to say.

"I'm fine...but you're paying for this shit."

"What did you tell the cops?" "Don't get cussed out."

"I'm serious. I wanna know what you said."

"Fuck you, Blake. I'm on Washington and Kostner. Send somebody to get me right the fuck now."

"Yup."

"And if they don't show me at least a hundred grand I'm not even getting in the car."

"Deal."

"Bitch," Barbie said and hung up.

Blake chuckled and hit the stop button on his second iPhone.

He had recorded the whole conversation, thinking that he might need it one day in court.

He gave Bubbles $100,000 cash and the keys to one of his foreign cars and sent her to pick up Barbie.

Unbeknownst to them he and Nona would be 30,000 in the air on his Gulfstream jet by the time they made it back to the mansion.

He stuck around just long enough for his doctor to stop by and swab his mouth for DNA. Tiff-Tiff gave Dr. Jacobi the address to her mom's apartment and he promised to bill Blake for the trip.

Then Blake took Nona with him to the airport. They boarded his private jet, ate crab cakes and buttery crab legs, popped bottles of Ace of Spades champagne, and listened to Bulletface's latest hits.

His daughter wanted him there in Hollywood with her, and Savaria's word was golden.

King Rio

Chapter 14

Pedro sat quietly in the backseat of his dark blue Rolls-Royce Phantom Drophead Coupe, calculating the cartel's newest drug shipment on his smartphone and trying his best not to keep looking over at Mary's luscious brown thighs.

She'd changed into the chic yellow minidress he'd had delivered to the bedroom she and Lisa had slept in at his Malibu mansion. It was a Valentino dress. He'd paid $31,000 for it.

Soothed by the alluring scent of the ocean, sitting next to a stunningly attractive African American woman with the most heartwarming smile this side of the border, Pedro felt that this moment was almost magical.

"What are you calculating?" Mary asked, staring at his smartphone. "Stocks," Pedro lied.

"What kind of stocks?"

"The kind that made Alexus rich."

"The kind that got her indicted on federal drug charges?" "I don't know anything about that."

"Hmm."

Pedro glanced over at Mary with a growing smile on his face. Dazzling rays of sunlight pouring in through the PhanEagleconvertible roof gave her an angelic appearance. She was as drop-dead gorgeous as any top model.

"Where are you taking me, Pedro?" She turned and stared out her window at the rolling waves of the ocean waters as Sergio, the driver, cruised up Pacific Coast Highway. "I'm telling you now, if you shoot one more person the deal is off. I'm taking my money and going home."

Pedro chuckled.

"I don't see what's funny." Mary gave him the side eye.

"It's funny because you're treating me like the bad guy. I saved your friend's life in Juarez. I saved Blake's life in Chicago. You should be thanking me. I know Bulletface is like a god to you Black people."

Mary sucked her teeth. "He's alright. I wouldn't go that far as to say he's a god. He's a great rapper. I like his music."

"Sounds to me like you're a hater."

"Oh, please." Mary rolled her sexy brown eyes and popped her sexy plump lips. A half-smirk illuminated her pretty face. Pedro had no idea what kind of perfume she had on but it smelled delicious and had his penis throbbing in his finely tailored Hartmarx slacks.

He had a grand breakfast planned for the two of them at The Griddle Cafe on Sunset Boulevard. Lisa was invited but since she was far too hungover to do anything but vomit and sleep, it left just Pedro and Mary to enjoy the many wonders of a Hollywood morning.

"I can't lie," Mary said, "Bulletface is like my favorite rapper— besides Tupac, of course. And I absolutely love Alexus. Queen A! Yassss!" She threw her hands up to the sky in excitement. "Alexus is that bitch, okay? She's young, fly, rich; she gives back to the poor and rebuilds lower-class communities; she has the cutest little baby boy and even takes care of Bulletface's daughter like she's her own child; she owns an entire entertainment corporation, including the number one TV network in the game; and the list goes on and on. Alexus is not to be fucked with. You see they had to try to bomb her in Indianapolis. Queen A bars none."

Pedro smiled proudly. "Yeah, my little cousin is something else." "She truly is. I hope I get to meet her one day. She's my idol."

Pedro nodded. "She's idolized in Mexico as well. Hundreds of thousands of little girls want to be like her."

"If I had her life I'd be the happiest girl alive. Even with being in a coma. At least I'd have a fine ass husband, and I'd be able to know for sure that my family was set for life."

Sergio, a big fan of Blake's, must have been listening to their conversation, because suddenly a Bulletface song featuring 50 Cent was playing from the Phantom's speakers.

'My bitch bad, my bitch hood Ten Bugattis, no Ace Hood
I woke up, got poled up
Get poled down if you ain't hood I'm so rich, no hoe shit
Ten figures, big bro shit
Wifey in the cut wit a hun'ed billion Tried to tell these niggas I own shit And y'all niggas ain't on shit
Tell me who yo boss, what's his net worth Wanna network, we

can network
> I got work on the set, show you how the set work Diss and
> I'ma let the Tec work
> Make the Tec burst until ya chest squirt
> Last nigga that dissed me got caught lackin' and got murked
> Thirty punch like Mayweather
> I'll start the heat like May weather I'm number one like that
> "A" letter
> If you know he hot, know I'm way better Bulletface 'bout
> straight cheddar...'

Mary's head moved back and forth to the beat of the music. Pedro wasn't a big fan of rap but for Mary he didn't mind. He went back to the calculations and figured he'd clear around $12 million off the kilos of cocaine that were now being loaded onto semitrailers in a San Francisco warehouse.

"Those numbers are unbelievable. Are you seeing that kind of money?" Mary asked. Her eyes were glued to Pedro's smartphone. She put a hand on his wrist to lower it to his knee so she could get a better view.

"Why?" His eyes found her cleavage and lingered there for several seconds before rising to her face.

"I'm curious," she said. "Curiosity killed the cat."

"Oh, whatever. Just answer the question. Is that money you're calculating?"

Pedro shrugged. "Might be. What's it to you?"

Mary let out a sigh and shook her head. "Why are you doing all this for me? I don't even know you, and you're blowing all your money on me like I'm somebody important. I don't get it."

"Maybe it's not for you to get. Maybe I'm just a nice guy." Pedro pocketed his smartphone and turned to Mary. He'd paid top dollar for two recent Paul Mitchell graduates to get her hair and makeup in order this morning, and the duo had pulled it off flawlessly. Now Mary looked even more beautiful than she had when Pedro first saw her at the bar.

"Is all this being done for some pussy?" she asked with a squint. "You might have done better just asking. All this extravagant shit ain't necessary."

"It's unladylike to talk that way." "Oh yeah?"

"Yeah. I like classy women. And if I wanted a prostitute I

77

could easily have gotten one." He straightened his tie and checked his watch. "You're thinking too much. Tell me more about you."

Just then, a black Jeep appeared from around the curve of the turn they were coming up on. It slowed a little. Its driver, a Hispanic woman wearing

dark sunglasses, flicked her eyes at the Phantom. So did her passenger, a heavyset Hispanic man in a camo shirt and Raiders cap.

The Jeep disappeared around the bend as quickly as it had appeared.

In the rearview mirror, Sergio locked eyes with Pedro. It was a fleeting look but it was enough to unsettle Pedro.

"Well," Mary began, "first and foremost, I'm not a prostitute. Nor am I the kind of girl who gets all wet and horny over a man's money. No matter how rich or famous you are, your money is yours at the end of the day."

A nervous chuckle blew from Pedro's throat. He put his briefcase on his lap and unlatched it, but he left it shut.

"Continue," he said.

"Like I told you in Juarez, I'm from Indianapolis. I was actually in town when Alexus got hurt at that hotel. That's the same day my cousin Bread got killed in Haughville. And I went to school with the girl who got killed at the hotel before the bombing."

"Lot of people" — Pedro touched a button between their seats and the convertible roof began to close — "get killed nowadays. It's sad. Just lost my own father, you know. Life's crazy."

He was looking over his right shoulder at the empty road behind them. In his periphery, he saw Sergio pull an Uzi submachine gun from under a newspaper on the passenger's seat.

"Something else you might wanna know about me is that I have school tomorrow," Mary went on, "and I'd truly appreciate it if you'd hurry up with this little 24-hour bribe date. This is some out of this world type shit but for the money you're paying I can't complain. I'm about to go and drop the down payment to get the new Impala with my half of the money. I'll buy and sell hair to flip whatever's left."

"You don't have to do that. I'll get you a car," Pedro offered.

"Why do you keep looking back there? You knew the people in

that Jeep or some—"

Suddenly, Mary gasped. Her eyes went wide.

The Jeep's driver must have made a U-turn; it was swinging around the bend at the turn Sergio had just made seconds prior, going much faster now. In no time it was twenty feet off their rear bumper.

"Step on it, Serg!" Pedro said.

He threw open his briefcase. There were two .40-caliber Glocks and four extended magazines laying atop neatly stacked packets of bank-new

hundred-dollar bills. He picked up both guns just as the convertible top closed. Sergio shut the windows.

"What's going on?" Mary asked. But she didn't need a reply.

The man in the Jeep hung out of the passenger window with an assault rifle, just as Sergio was passing a Chevron gas station on Pacific Coast Highway.

As the gunfire commenced, Mary yelped and ducked low in her seat. Pedro didn't even flinch.

He touched another button on the console between his and Mary's seat.

Two dozen spikes spilled out of the Phantom's rear end and scattered all across the road.

The Jeep lost all four tires and went sliding atop a shower of sparks into the Chevron gas pumps.

A second later the Jeep and the pump exploded into a plume of flames. Sergio slammed down on the gas pedal and raced off down the road. "The deal's off," Mary said as she sat up and gazed out her window at the

wreckage. "I am taking my black ass home."

King Rio

Chapter 15

Los Angeles, California

"I don't know if I should be sorry or excited to give you this news."

"Don't play with me."

"I'm not kidding. This is the kind of news that makes men."

"Don't make me hang up on yo old ass," Blake said into his Bluetooth headset. He was onstage at the Staples Center with his children, his MBM recording artists, and a team of music engineers, taking a break from a soundcheck for tonight's show.

The man he was talking to on the phone was Dr. Jacobi.

"You are the father," the doctor said. "I knew it when I saw him but the test makes it a hundred percent certain."

Blake looked down at his son and daughter; they were standing on either side of him, King eating a coconut donut, Vari sucking her thumb and holding a black Barbie doll.

Blake's wife had been pregnant before the Indianapolis hotel blast, but she'd lost the baby as a result of it. He'd always wanted another son. Ever

since King Neal was born, he'd wanted another boy to raise into a King, another little brother for Savaria.

He ended the call and completed the soundcheck, deciding he'd wait to tell Vari about her new brother. Tiff-Tiff was Vari's deceased mother's first cousin. He didn't know how he would break it to his baby girl that her cousin's son was actually her brother.

Nona tried keeping her distance from everyone out of respect for Alexus, choosing to stand at the far back of the stage with Meach's girlfriend.

Occasionally she stepped forward to give Biggs a drink of water or to dab beads of sweat from his face. She was so thick and pretty-faced that Blake couldn't help glancing her way every couple of seconds. He wished Nona would step over and dab the sweat from his face, but his assistant— Kendall, a buxom white woman he'd met in Miami Beach— kept him refreshed and hydrated.

They went over the 12 songs he'd be performing with other MBM artists and the 9 he'd do solo. Some of them were classics, from the infamous "Three Kings" to his favorite new banger "Drill Season". Three special guests — Kevin Gates, Lil Boosie, and Twista— would be making surprise appearances for a couple of bonus performances.

Blake was back to doing what he did best: performing his music in front of crowds of ecstatic Bulletface fans. He loved the industry more than he liked to admit. He was averaging $1.9 million per concert. Sure, there were ups and downs, but for the most part he had a blast at every show. In just a couple of years, he'd managed to make an unprecedented rise to the very top of the rap game. His love life hadn't worked out like he'd hoped it would, and he'd lost several friends and family members along the way, but all in all he couldn't complain.

With a net worth of over $1 billion, he was simultaneously the king of rap and the king of the dope game. As his close friend Meek Mill had once told him, Bulletface was the face of the streets. He was the ultimate American dream come true for street niggas.

"We can't ever stop doin' this shit," Meek had said. Blake agreed wholeheartedly.

After the soundcheck, everyone left the stadium and met back up at Blake's Malibu mansion a few hours later. During the ride home in his Mercedes Sprinter van, Blake enjoyed a long talk with his kids. He'd missed them. Especially Vari's sharp tongue and King's cantankerous expressions.

Kendall got in a word or two when she could. She told him to get ready to do three radio interviews over the phone to promote tonight's concert. He had a paid club appearance after the concert at Club Avalon that would make him an additional $110,000.

He sent a text message to Bubbles telling her to get Tiff-Tiff and her son on a plane to Los Angeles as soon as possible. Bubbles replied saying she and Barbie were already on their way to the airport but that she would head back for Tiff and send for the kid.

Nona caught him alone in the bathroom when they all made it inside. She stood off to the side of him and watched him relieve his bladder.

"I missed that big ol' thang," she said, reaching out to touch his dick as he shook out the last couple of drops of urine. "Thanks for giving us that money last night. I definitely needed it to pay some bills. Biggs so fuckin' stingy with his lil money."

"He earned it. He got the right to be tight with it. It's his money." Blake flushed the toilet, washed his hands, and dried them on one of his custom designed bath towels.

"Nuh uh," Nona countered, "I took care of that nigga when he got out the joint. Now he's a millionaire and acts like he forgot who helped his ungrateful ass get there."

"I got you, baby." Blake filled his palms with Nona's pillowy butt cheeks and have her a kiss. "Let bruh do him. It ain't his job to take care of you.

That's my job."

"Mmm hmm." Nona rolled her eyes as he began kissing the side of her neck. "You sure wasn't trying to take care of me when you got back with Alexus."

"That's old shit. Me and Lexi ain't even together no more."

"Well, what about you and that bitch Barbie? You sent that bitch a hundred thousand dollars."

"To keep that lawsuit off my back." "What the fuck ever."

"Didn't I buy you a Jag? And a house?" Blake grinned at her. "Forgot about that, huh?"

"I ain't forgot shit." "Sounds like it."

"Well, I didn't,"she said, rolling her eyes.

Her attitude was turning Blake on. His hands— strong and replete with bulging veins— massaged her soft ass. She had on an orange dress that embraced her every curve, and her hair was laid for the gods with orange highlights. Even her lips were painted a sparkling orange. The yellow diamond ring on her right hand's ring finger had been a gift from Blake two years prior. The yellow diamond tennis bracelet on her wrist had also been a gift from him. He was glad to see she still had them.

When they made it out to the game room where everyone was gathered, he sat Vari on one knee and King on the other. Vari laid her head on his shoulder and sucked her thumb until he grabbed her wrist and made her stop sucking it. She was obviously sleepy; her eyelids were fluttering, struggling to stay open.

King, on the other hand (or "knee", to be more precise), was as energetic as ever as he explained the many uses of peanut butter to

Nona, who stood quietly at Blake's side.

"I put it on my pancakes," he was saying, "on my jelly sand-wiches, on my, um, my ice cream, on my bread regular, on my toast bread in the morning, in my oatmeal..."

Biggs and Meach were playing the latest 2K basketball game on the PS4 game console. Meach had the Clippers; Curry was dominating.

Will Scrill was sitting on the pool table, talking on his smartphone and rolling a blunt while sipping some Lean.

Kendall was on a beanbag with her laptop, sending emails, replying to emails, and doing all the other things she did for Blake every day.

These were the days Blake cherished. There was nothing like relaxing with family and friends in a ridiculously large home, getting prepared to go out and make even more money. He'd grown up poor, in a lower-class neighborhood full of dope dealers and drug addicts. His father had been strung out on crack; his mother had been an alcoholic. He himself had followed in his brother's footsteps by joining the crowd of dealers, only he was a hundred times more violent than Streets had ever been.

Now he was the infamous Bulletface.

Things could not have possibly turned out better.

He looked at King and placed his hand over the little guy's mouth. "If you say peanut butter one more time it's gon' be me and you," he
threatened. He pushed King off his lap. "Go play."

King crossed his arms and pouted. He was picture-perfect in an all-white Gucci outfit.

"How come you didn't make Vari get off your leg, too?"

"Because she's going to sleep. Because she's not talking about peanut butter. Shall I continue?"

King poked his bottom lip out.

"Is that supposed to make me feel bad?" Blake asked. "Be-cause it doesn't."

"You're mean, Daddy."

"He really is, ain't he?" Nona picked King up and put him on her hip. "Don't mind him. Your dad is the Grinch."

King's eyes got wide, and he snickered. "Like the Grinch that

84

took Christmas?"

Nona nodded her head yes and King Neal cracked up laughing.

"Come on," Nona said, turning to leave. "We can make us some peanut butter sandwiches. And ya daddy can't get none."

"Haaa ha, haaa ha, we're making peanut butter sandwiches and you can't get none," King teased as Nona carried him away.

Blake laughed and shook his head. Vari was already fast asleep on his leg.

He got up and carried her to his bedroom. She didn't awaken as he pulled the covers up to her chin and planted a kiss on her forehead.

He went back to the game room and participated in two of the three scheduled radio interviews. The third would be done within the next hour or so.

He was getting ready to head to the kitchen to see what King and Nona were up to when Pedro Costilla waltzed into the room with Enrique's corpulent son Sergio and a sexy dark-skinned girl Blake had never seen.

The look on Pedro's face put a modicum of worry in Blake's mind. "Can I have a word with you in the hallway?" Pedro asked.

Blake frowned and trailed Pedro out into the hallway. He heard the girl whisper, "Oh, my God, it's really Bulletface! And look— Meach and Biggs!"

Alone in the hall with Pedro, Blake leaned his back against the wall and wished he'd brought a cup of Lean to the chat.

"Somebody sent a hit my way this morning," Pedro said, lighting a cigar. "They put a few holes in my Phantom. Was heading to breakfast when it happened."

"The fuck am I supposed to do about that?" Blake asked.

"You're supposed to do something. Boss man. I saved your fucking life last night and just about lost mine in the process. The least you could do is make sure I'm safe here in California."

"How in the fuck am I supposed to do that? Like I knew they was coming for you. And how did you happen to pop up right when some niggas was shootin' at me?"

"The Latin Kings were paid to take you out by the same guys who came after me this morning. They're practically an offshoot of the Sinaloa cartel."

"Ain't they wit' us?"

"Yeah, and so are the Zetas, but there are some who don't appreciate the fact that a black guy's in charge now. Plus, El Chapo's loyal soldiers didn't join forces with us when everyone else in the Sinaloa cartel did. I wouldn't be surprised if Gamuza himself is behind all these hits."

Blake's expression became quizzical.

"Gamuza was the boss of the Zeta cartel," Pedro explained. "He cut off my grandfather's head with a chainsaw."

Blake nodded. "Papi told me that story."

"Yeah, well, Gamuza's a very old man now. He's in his nineties, I believe. I think it's kind of hard for him to accept you being in charge while Alexus is out of commission. That may be why those men were after you last night."

The smoke from Pedro's cigar was irritating Blake's eyes. He took a step to the side and waved the smoke away, trying to think of a solution to the problems at hand.

He wished he could just stand in front of Gamuza and put a bullet in the old man's head.

"Where the fuck is Gamuza?" he asked finally.

"I don't know. Probably somewhere in Juarez. I've only met him once, when my father made the deal to merge the top cartels. Hardly anyone has ever laid eyes on him. The only thing I know for certain is that he's in Mexico, and that he's not happy with you."

Blake didn't know what to say to that. It was kind of shocking to hear that the world's most feared Mexican drug cartel boss hated him. Just five years ago Blake had been a nobody, a crack dealer in a hood full of crack dealers, a baby's daddy in a neighborhood full of baby's daddies. The reality of his life now was almost too much to bear.

"But to the shipment," Pedro said, changing the subject. "Twenty-four thousand kilos. Most already spoken for. We've got your list of what you want going to your guys. Are we still doing business with Cup and the Vice Lords in Chicago?"

"Of course."

Nodding his head, Pedro's attention shifted to his smartphone. He typed a long text message.

While Pedro typed, Blake glanced up the hallway at Nona,

who was heading his way with King walking alongside her. Each of them had a sandwich and a cold glass of milk.

Blake motioned for Nona to go into the game room and wait for him. As bad as he wanted to take her to bed for some good loving— or to any place, for that matter —he knew that he had to take care of business first.

Pedro said: "Doctors told Rita that Alexus might be out of the coma within the next couple of weeks. That lawyer of hers has already talked to the judge. Bond will probably be set at thirty or forty million. She'll spend some weeks recuperating but she'll make it through alright. I suggest you get all your fun in now. You know she's not going to just let you keep fucking around on her when she regains her strength."

"Fuck that. She pulled a gun on me," Blake said. "As far as I'm concerned I'm single."

"Yeah, yeah, yeah. Say that when she sends Enrique to murder every whore you fuck. I'd like to see you say it then."

Blake waved off the threat. He didn't have time to be listening to Pedro's bullshit. Lately he'd been thinking of starting a music streaming service, and now was the perfect time to hire a team to begin the research. Kendall would have it done in no time.

When he and Pedro were done talking business, Blake took Nona out to his Sprinter van.

The van rocked and swayed for close to an hour.

King Rio

Chapter 16

A vicious slap to the face awakened Porsche from a drunken stupor. Last night she and Sasha had finished the night off with two bottles of
Remy Martin, Xanax bars, blunts of Kush, and a few grams of coke.

The slap was just enough to compel her heavy eyelids to creep open. "Bitch, get the fuck up!"

She saw Glo's face, felt his hand wrap tightly around the front of her neck, and suddenly she was airborne.

Her forehead struck the corner of their bedroom door. She looked up at Glo, stunned. Blood spilled down her face.

Her heart drummed with fear.

She didn't know what she had done to infuriate Glo to the point of violence, but she knew one thing: Glo was a killer. He was a savage in the streets, a gunslinger of high-powered weapons. His reputation was the reason he'd been chosen to be a high-ranking leader of the gang.

The ache of her lacerated forehead made her double over in pain. Blood was running into her mouth. She could smell it dripping from her nose.

"Don't ever try to manipulate me like that. Bitch. You got a problem with that nigga it's yo problem." He walked calmly out of the bedroom and returned seconds later with a thick yellow towel that he quickly tossed onto Porsche's face. "Go clean that blood up and get the fuck out."

The pain was unbearable. Porsche rocked and cried like a baby, holding the towel to her head. Within seconds most of the yellow was red and dripping.

Suddenly gentle and civilized, Glo clamped a hand on her forearm and lifted her to her feet. She wanted to resist his touch, to hurt him for hurting her, but the overwhelming throb in her head needed medical attention.

Glo walked her to the bathroom and gave her a weak shove toward the sink.

"Sasha!" she cried out.

"Fuck is you callin' her for? What, you think she gon' help you?" Glo was lingering by the doorway. He had a gun with an extended clip in one hand. His voice was as frigid as ice. "Lucky I ain't wack yo li'l goofy ass. What if I would've caught a murder case fuckin' around out there? I don't even know that nigga Bulletface. Shit, I still might have a body after what went down. Stupid ass bitch."

Porsche cut on the cold water, dropped the blood-soaked towel in the sink, and splashed her stinging forehead.

The blood continued to spill. She could not see through all the blood and water. She heard an unfamiliar voice say, "Glo, come on, big folks. Let's slide. Fuck that bitch."

Seconds later Porsche heard Lil Durk's "500 Homicides" — Glo's favorite song as of lately — blasting from his SUV as he drove off down the alley.

Porsche managed to lift her head a moment later, and the deep gash she saw in the reflection of the oval mirror over her sink was enough to make a person faint.

It was on the right side of her forehead, a gaping slit on top of a knot. She knew right away that it needed stitches.

There was blood all down the chest of her shirt, all over her hands and neck, and a lot was still running down her face. She got a fresh towel from the hallway closet and pressed it to her forehead before getting her smartphone from the bedroom and calling Sasha.

"Get over here!" she sobbed into the phone when Sasha finally picked up. "This nigga Glo done busted my head! You gotta get me to the hospital."

It was a good thing that Sasha lived right next door. When she stormed into the living room, Porsche had the keys to her Range Rover in one hand and was using her other hand to hold the towel to her head.

"Girl, what happened? Did he hit you? Bitch, where is yo' gun at? You should've popped his ol' bitch ass, nigga wanna hit on a girl."

Sasha was obviously hungover; the grogginess in her voice was unmistakable, and she had on her bed clothes— tiny gray boy shorts and and a Glo Gang tee shirt. Instead of shoes she had on slippers. Her hair was tied up in a Gucci scarf.

Porsche went to the bedroom and got her purse and a large

suitcase, and Sasha helped her out to the Range Rover and into the passenger seat.

"Let me drive," Sasha said, as if that hadn't already been Porsche's unspoken suggestion. She put the suitcase in the backseat and ran around to the driver's door. She started the engine and sped off without another word.

As Sasha was turning out of the alleyway, she and Porsche witnessed a coldblooded murder.

Porsche saw the boy first.

He was on her side of the SUV, walking down the street with his head down, looking at his smartphone.

By the time Sasha looked at him, another boy whose head was halfway hidden in a light blue hoodie came running across the street in the smartphone-watcher's direction.

The boy in the hoodie pulled a gun out of his hoodie's belly pocket and shot the boy with the smartphone three times.

One of the bullets hit the boy in the head.

It happened in an instant, but to Porsche it seemed like slow motion.

Sasha screamed, "Oh, shit! Shit!" She straightened the wheel, accelerated down the alley across from them, and didn't slow down until they were four blocks away from the scene of the murder.

"I need to move the fuck away from these crazy ass niggas!" Porsche exclaimed. There were tears in her eyes, but not from witnessing the murder; it felt like someone was driving a nail into her skull.

"Oh, my God, I can't believe that. I know that boy. That was Boo Man who got shot. Shit," Sasha said. She sounded frantic. "Leery me just get you to this hospital. Shit, shit, shit."

Porsche studied her forehead in the visor mirror. "I'm gon' kill that nigga, Sash. On my momma's grave, the next time I see that nigga he's dead meat."

King Rio

Chapter 17

'I'm back to trappin' like I used to do

I'm filthy rich but ask about me hoe I used to shoot I just went and bought the newest coupe

That new Bugatti cost me $3.5 and that's the truth So mothafuck what haters got to say

I got a billion in the bank, that's all I got to say Ain't never slippin', no, I got a K

He disrespect me, soon's I catch him, know I gotta spray I used to ride 'round wit' that nina, nigga

Now my bitch thick, look like I'm ridin' 'round wit' Serena, nigga...' Bulletface was onstage at the Staples Center.

Kevin Gates was onstage with him.

Together the two were performing "I Used To Trap", a trap banger that currently had the streets on lock nationwide.

When he completed his verse, Blake went backstage to change into a white True Religion and Louis Vuitton outfit for his performance of "Free Guwop". It was a song he held dear to his heart, since it was written about Gucci Mane, the man who was his favorite trap rapper in Atlanta. From Blake's point of view as the number one drug pusher in the country, it was only right to keep the trap god's name in the people's minds while he was

away in federal prison. Blake put on two white diamond necklaces that had stones as big as quarters and heavy, diamond-flooded MBM pendants. The chains matched his brilliantly shining Hublot watch, bracelet, pinkie rings, and earrings.

He took a bathroom break while Gates performed "John Gotti" solo.

Exiting the bathroom, he ran into Bubbles and Barbie, who'd flown in to LAX just in time for the show. They were standing with Nona and Biggs. All three of the girls had put on pearl white minidresses to match the outfit Blake has told them he would be leaving in. He'd paid for the dresses, the Louboutin heels, and the brand-new, white croc skin Birkin bags that they were now rocking.

"I'm loving this backstage action," Bubbles said, smiling and constantly flicking her eyes from Barbie to Blake, as if sensing that soon he would be assaulting Barbie again.

"We at Avalon after this," Blake said. "The ride gon' be turnt, too. I got a new tour bus, that bitch got stripper poles and e'rything." He grinned, showcasing his bling.

Barbie didn't look at him; She kept her eyes on her iPhone. Her hair was in a different style than it had been last time he'd seen her, and he guessed it was because they had to chop some off to put in the staples, which were perfectly hidden beneath a comb-over.

Bubbles blew him a kiss.

Nona gave him a hug and whispered, "Go out there and put on for the streets, bae. You're the king. They love you."

Her encouraging words stuck with him as he made his way back out to the stage. He'd taken the kids back to Rita's mansion earlier; it was going on 10:00 pm now.

"Time to take over the night," he said aloud to himself. He repeated the phrase several times before he made his return from behind a stage curtain to the crowd of over 18,000 fans.

The beat to "Free Guwop", a tribute to Gucci Mane off Bulletface's Goon Muzik 3 mixtape, started booming throughout the stadium. The fans chanted the beginning of the song in unison, while Bulletface paced the stage and held the mic out to their screams.

Then he went in:

'Free Wop, free Wop...

Free Wop, pussy nigga, free Wop

I say mothafuck the cop...who locked up Wop Free Wop, pussy nigga, free Wop

I'm so icy, all these chains I got a lot Gold mouf, full o' diamonds, jackpot Try to jack me, better clap me

Cause this choppa chop like Jet Li

And the clip in my new Glock look like a mop Bulletface, he got the game on lock

In the safe, I got them thangs, whole pies Gimme twenty for the brick

Just don't think that this a lick

Try the king and you gon' get the whole 9 Look at all these chains on me, rings on me Pull up in the trap, all the fiends on me Smell like Kush smoke and Lean on me

If my nigga fall off, he can lean on me Cop pull me over, all I got is Lean on me "You smoke crack, don't cha" Lean On Me

Done made e'ry dope fiend on the scene OD You ain't seen no G's till you seen my niggas In the club iced out smokin mean OG

I say free my nigga Guwop

Tell the judge I'll put up two blocks Where I'm from my niggas shoot cops Like they some kin to Tupac...'

It was at that very moment that Blake noticed a face in the crowd. Draya Michelle.

She was in the first row to the left of the stage, looking sexy as she always did in a simple white Bulletface shirt over small denim short-shorts.

Pedro, Sergio, and two women — the Black girl he'd brought to the mansion and a Hispanic girl— were in the same row.

Blake was glad that he'd chosen to put on his most expensive diamond jewelry for this set. He'd done it to pay homage to Guwop, but now it came in handy for another reason — to impress the lovely Draya.

He hoped the $8 million his jewelry was worth would do the trick.

The thoughts of a good time with Draya were fleeting; Lil Boosie came out to perform "On Some Gangsta Shit" with Blake, and suddenly Draya's

face was no longer Blake's main priority.

"On Some Gangsta Shit" was a favorite of Blake's, mainly because the chorus was chopped and screwed.

He sailed effortlessly into his verse:

You see, I came here tryna chill

Please don't make me get on some gangsta shit

Try to snatch my chain and watch how quick I get on some gangsta shit I be ridin' around, bumpin' UGK on some gangsta shit

I be ridin' around, bumpin' UGK on some gangsta shit 'Nigga, don't make me get on that gangsta shit

Pull up and stank a bitch

All these niggas wit me totin' straps wit thirty in the clips

If you got bread but no respect, they'll come and take yo shit

You owe some bread, if you got legs, they'll come and break yo shit Street niggas...that's all I hang around

People say put down the guns, but we can't put our bangers

down 'Cause if you get into it, you bet' not play around

These young niggas ain't playin' 'round, they gon' make you lay it down Like Ball and G, my partners all some G's

I say mothafuck a drought, Bulletface got all the keys I caught some cases, but never said a word

Had my nigga off the witness, threw lil bruh a couple birds Yeah, we winnin'...my clique like Charlie Sheen

Pullin' all the porn stars and the models for the team A mob figure, it's money over bitches

If we find out you been snitchin' then it's probably over witcha...'

The large diamonds in Bulletface and Boosie's jewelry made it known that the two of them were filthy rich, in case someone in the crowd didn't already know it, and the true stories in their lyrics made it known that they were real life gangsters, which everyone more than likely already knew.

Well, not everyone.

Evidently, someone had not gotten the memo.

Two songs later, as Bulletface and Biggs were performing "Drill Season", a skinny black boy in a plaid button up shirt leapt up onto the stage and snatched one of Blake's diamond necklaces.

It happened so quickly that at first Blake didn't know that his chain had been snatched.

Then, realizing it, he jumped into the crowd and chased the boy down. He didn't know Biggs was there with him until he caught the boy by the collar and punched him in the jaw; Biggs swung at the same time and caught the chain-snatcher in the left eye.

The guy went down.

Blake took his chain from the unconscious man's hand, and he and Biggs made their triumphant return to the stage.

MBM's DJ restarted the "Drill Season" beat. The crowd applauded and cheered.

Draya shouted: "I love you, Bulletface!"

Security escorted the chain-snatcher out of the building. And the show went on.

Chapter 18

Jacob Stalling had an eye that was swollen shut and a broken jaw but he wasn't as upset about it as most men would be. He was a 19-year-old college dropout from Compton with a pregnant girlfriend and no job to support either one of them.

So yesterday morning when he was approached by Charles Mack, the biggest drug-dealer in Compton, at the Azteca Barber Shop on Compton Boulevard, he'd had good reason to get excited.

Charles Mack had always taken a liking to young Jacob. For one, both of them were Bloods, and for two, they were both born and raised in Compton.

Jacob needed money.

Charles Mack had a ton of money.

"You see this?" Charles had said, pulling a ticket out of his pants pocket. "This is a ticket to tomorrow's Bulletface concert at the Staples Center.

Know who he is?"

"Who doesn't know who Bulletface is?" had been Jake's hasty reply. "He's, like, the new Jay Z. Nigga got a billion."

"Yeah, well, those chains he always wears at his concerts are worth a lot of money. A lot. A whole lot. You feelin' me?"

Jake had nodded in the affirmative. He was feeling Charles so far.

"If you can snatch one of those chains and get it to me, I'll pay you ten grand. Maybe even fifteen. What do you think?"

Of course Jake had agreed. He would go to the the Bulletface concert, snatch the billionaire rapper's necklace, and make off with enough cash to get himself a car and move his girlfriend out of her aunt's decrepit old basement.

Now, as he was being carried out of the stadium's rear exit by four burly Hispanic men, he was almost happy. He may not have escaped with the chain, but he knew all those smartphones had captured his attempt to get it. He'd be on World Star by midnight. He'd be on TMZ tomorrow. Hell, Charles Mack would probably still look out for him for the bold chain- snatching attempt. Maybe Charles would put him on, give him a way to make some big money to support the kid he had on the way. Maybe he'd be able to sue Bulletface for knocking him out. The possibilities were endless.

But then a powerful arm curled around the front of his neck, and the men carrying him slammed him face-first into the concrete.

"Stop resisting!" one of the men shouted.

"I'm not resisting!" is what Jake tried to say, but he only managed to get the "I" out.

"Stop fucking resisting!" It was the same voice.

Then a second voice whispered in his ear: "How dare you try to steal from the richest fucking gangster on the planet. Are you retarded or something?

Huh? Are you fucking slow? How dare you try to steal from the fucking Costilla Cartel!"

"I...I can't breathe," Jake said. Those were his last and final words.

The man choking Jacob Stalling did not let up until the 19-year-old was dead.

Chapter 19

"I want them all dead," Porsche said as she and Sasha left out of the emergency room's double doors. "Every last one of them."

Sasha had fallen asleep in the waiting area while Porsche got her forehead stitched shut, and she was seemed to be sleepwalking as they made their way to the Range Rover.

As far as Porsche's mood went, "pissed" was an understatement. She didn't understand why Glo had suddenly changed his views toward Blake

and quite frankly she didn't care. Now she wanted him in a grave too. "You still ain't told me what it is you did to make that man hit you like

that," Sasha said sleepily.

"You gon' make me hit you if you let some more dumb shit fall out yo' mouth like you just did," Porsche snapped.

They were crossing the parking lot.

Sasha sucked her teeth. "Bitch, I'm just sayin'. Tell me what the fuck went down. Don't leave me in the dark if I'm gon' be all up in the play. Them niggas ain't to be played with. We gotta be dead ass serious if we got a problem with them. Or else we'll end up like Boo Man."

Porsche thought long and hard before she spoke. By then they were in the Range, this time with her in the driver's seat.

She'd gotten a Pepsi from a vending machine in the hospital. So had Sasha. They drank their sodas and listened to a Dej Loaf song on the radio.

"Somehow," Porsche said finally, "Blake talked Glo n'em out of getting at him. Or somebody did. I'm not sure who. Glo was mad at me for talking him into extortin' Blake in the first place. That's why he busted my head. He said I tricked him into making my problem his."

She paused and looked back at the suitcase in the backseat. Sasha turned and looked at it too.

Then Porsche drove off.

"I'm still gon' get that nigga Blake taken care of. Believe that. Alexus too. Fuck the bullshit. Glo's ass is on my list now, but I'll handle him later." She looked at the suitcase again, this time through the rearview mirror. "In fact, I already took care of Glo.

Trust me, his ass will be in a lot more pain than I am when he goes home."

"Bitch, what did you do?" Again Sasha looked back at the suitcase. "Should I open that to take a look for myself?"

"Go right ahead." Porsche smiled.

Sasha climbed over to the backseat and unzipped the suitcase. Opening it, she gasped in shock.

Inside the suitcase lay four cellophane wrapped kilos of a tan powdery substance, two big bags of loud-smelling marijuana, and a bunch of rubber- banded stacks of cash.

"Bitch, is this Glo's stuff?" Sasha asked.

Porsche nodded yes, still smiling. "Sure in the fuck is. That's all the dope and money he got to his name too. Fuck that nigga, I'm keeping all that shit.

And I still got big money in the bank. We can go to another city and meet some new niggas. If you want your parents to move out there with us I'll get them a house and pay the first three months of rent. We can be some brand- new bitches, you feel me? We can move to Indianapolis, St. Louis, Milwaukee — wherever you wanna go."

Sasha took a moment to reply. She was flipping through the piles of cash. "How much money is this? And is this heroin or coke?"

"That's heroin. And last I checked that was $157,000 and some change.

It's more than enough for us to do our thang. We can get us a condo, I'll get you a car, we can do us, you feel me?"

For a full minute Sasha was dead silent. Porsche knew the teenager was thinking about the money. Little did Sasha know, Porsche had $500,000 in one bank account and almost $710,000 in another. She also had a hair salon that a cousin managed and operated for her. The savings had come from her maternal half-sister Mercedes Costilla and Mercedes's paternal half-sister Alexus.

"We gotta get my momma and daddy out of there quick, girl," Sasha said. "Glo will kill them if he finds out we stole his money."

"You still ain't said where you wanna move to," Porsche said.

"I got family in Gary." Sasha climbed back over to the passenger seat. "My grandma Dez lives out there."

"Gary? Nuh uh, bitch. It's bad as Chicago out there."

"My cousin Talisha lives in Miami. She's in the military. We could move there. Or we could really stay here in Chicago, just move to one of them nice neighborhoods where all the white people live. Didn't you say Mercedes was coming to live with you when she get out the hospital? She'll need a good environment to heal up. And shit, who knows, I might meet me a doctor or somethin' out there. One thing for certain, we gotta get the hell outta Englewood if we plan on keepin' Glo's money. I'm not about to play no games with them niggas."

Porsche thought it over.

She stopped at a McDonald's restaurant drive-thru and ordered two crispy chicken and bacon Premium McWraps. Sasha got a Big Mac and fries.

They sat in the parking lot and ate.

"You'll have to get a different truck," Sasha said. "Don't wanna get hit up in traffic. You know they won't be asking no questions."

Porsche nodded. "I'll trade it in, get me a black one."

"What kinda car you gon' get me?" "Whatever kind you want."

"Really? Any kind?" Sasha sounded a little too excited.

"Wait," Porsche said. "Any kind of car in your price range. We'll split that money and you buy whatever kind of car you want. Get you a Tahoe or somethin', or a short-body Benz."

Sasha's face lit up at the thought of her owning a Benz. "Okay, I'm all in.

Fuck it. Let's go," she said.

When they finished eating, Porsche hit the highway and headed out west. She knew the perfect person to sell the kilos of heroin to.

King Rio

Chapter 20

'Catchin' plays, catchin' plays
I woke up feelin' like I was on the moon
I woke up feelin' like I need a hundred goons
Look at the flicka da wrist, look at the flicka da wrist Look at the flicka da wrist, look at the flicka da wrist Look at the flicka da wrist, look at the flicka da wrist That wrist, look at the flicka da wrist
That wrist, look at the flicka da wrist

I woke up feelin' like I was on the moon
I woke up feelin' like I need a hundred goons Some niggas in my sleep tried to capture me Some bitches in my section tryna fuck for free Catch a play on these niggas, touchdown
I'm my own quarterback, put my team on Luxury, that's all I see
Look at the flicka da wrist, got 'em on me I don't see niggas, I don't see niggas
California loud, got me lit, nigga
I'm the shit, nigga, take your bitch, nigga
You better duck, fool, or you'll get hit, nigga...'
The Bulletface tour bus was the place to be if you were a celebrity in Los Angeles.

With Chedda Da Connect's hit single blaring from every speaker, and Draya Michelle teaching the girls how to properly make their asses clap on the stripper poles, and dozens of gold bottles and Kush blunts being passed around the crowded bus, a good time was being had by everyone.

Boosie and Kevin Gates was at the table with Bulletface, iced out like kings and laughing about the chain-snatching incident.

Biggs, Meach, and Will Scrill were also at the table, as well as YG, Young Jeezy, and Chris Brown. They were rolling blunts, smoking blunts, sipping Lean, passing out Molly and Xanax pills to the twentysome girls who'd joined them on the tour bus after the concert, and surfing social media on their smartphones.

Boosie told Bulletface all about life in prison, a place Bulletface hired he'd never experience, though he was more than ready for anything that came his way.

He told Bulletface stories about Pimp C, a rapper who Bulletface had never gotten the chance to meet but had always admired.

Then they made it to Avalon, and all the girls rushed off the bus and into the lavish Hollywood nightclub.

Blake was slower to exit the tour bus; he got a text from Pedro saying to call him immediately, so he stayed back with his MBM artists to make the call while everyone else headed inside.

"We've got trouble, Blake. Big trouble," Pedro said. "Trouble?" Blake looked at Meach. "What kind of trouble?"

"The kind that guarantees problems in Los Angeles, which is where we all are, am I right."

Blake say down at the table. "Man, just tell me what the fuck kinda trouble we got now."

"That guy who snatched your chain. He was a Blood from Compton.

Jacob Stalling was his name." "So muhfuckin what?"

"He's dead. My guys, uh...accidentally killed him when restraining him following that little incident."

Blake's mouth dropped open. He looked from Biggs to Meach, from Meach to Young, and finally to Scrill. "How in the fuck did he die?" He sailed on without giving Pedro time to reply. "Shit, I ain't got nothing to do with that. He was alive after I hit him."

The tour bus became so silent that a Young's zipper could be heard going up as he stepped out of the bathroom.

Biggs said, "That nigga dead?"

Blake nodded. He was just as shocked by the news as the gang was. "LAPD wants you for questioning," Pedro continued. "Call Britney, have

her figure it out. Just don't go off into any parties where they can easily find you until then, because you can bet they have an all-points bulletin out for you right this moment. They're gonna want a statement, that's all. Because it started with you, ya know. Oh, and the guy was a Blood from Compton. I hear they're not happy about losing him. Be safe out here, Blake."

Blake looked out the tour bus's darkly tinted rightside window at Avalon and shook his head in disbelief.

"My luck ain't shit." He picked an obese blunt of Haze out of his ashtray and lit it.

Next to the ashtray lay a 9 millimeter Glock with a thirty-round clip. Stacked up on the other side of the ashtray were eight piles of hundred- dollar bills and an AK-47 with a 100-round double-drum magazine. There was $410,000 altogether, just enough for Blake to enjoy himself tonight.

"The media will be all over this," Pedro said. "I suggest you lay low. Fly out to Cuba right this minute, like Assata Shakur did back in 1984. You're rich as shit. Nobody will be able to touch all the money you have in the Cayman Islands, which is most of your cash last I checked."

Blake frowned. "How you know all about my money?"

He hadn't told anyone but Alexus that he'd transferred $950 million of his money to the Cayman Islands early last July. Once he'd learned that it could not be touched by the American government under any circumstances, and that it was all untaxable, he'd made the transfer.

"I've got my sources," Pedro said

"What kinda sources? Look, I don't give a fuck about none of this shit you talkin' 'bout. I'm stepping in this club, and I'm gon' have fun like I always do wit' my niggas. I'll hit you later." Blake hit "end" with aggression and looked up at the guys.

All eyes were on him.

"The nigga died?" Biggs repeated.

"Yup." Blake picked up a pile of cash, put it to his ear, and said: "All I hear is the money. Fuck the world. Pack up them straps and we in this bitch." Again he looked out at the club.

The line stretched for four blocks. There were women and men, all eager to get in Avalon to see him and his artists.

Celebrities were being ushered in as they drove up. Gabrielle Union and

D. Wade, Jay Z and Beyoncé, Kim, her Kardashian sisters, and Kanye. Serena and Venus. Paris Hilton, Jada Pinkett and Will Smith.

Blake's assistant, who'd gone in with everyone else, sent him a text as he was packing the cash back into his duffle bag.

It read: 'Club owner just wired the $110,000 to your PayPal. Are you ready?'

He texted back: 'Omw in now.'

He stuffed the cash and the handgun in his duffle. He and the guys walked off the tour bus to a wave of excited screams.

"Bulletface!"

"MBM in the building!"

"Bulletface, can I please get a picture with you?" "Biggs! Meach! Scrill!"

Blake didn't stop to chat or take pics. He was thinking about what Pedro had just told him about the chain-snatcher's alleged ties to the Bloods.

A bouncer led them inside and up to the VIP area. People in the club began chanting "Bull-et-face!" again and again. There were already twenty bottles of Ace of Spades waiting for the MBM crew's tables, and Blake immediately ordered a hundred more for the other celebrities and their entourages.

He put on a pair of Louis Vuitton sunglasses and a gleaming smile to conceal the fact that he was scanning the club area downstairs.

Pedro's warning had him on edge.

He kept his duffle bag open under his table and told the hang to keep an eye on it add he ventured out to shake hands and mingle with the other celebrities. Kanye was without a doubt his favorite in the bunch. He thought the guy was a genius. They'd worked together on numerous occasions, and each time the results had been phenomenal.

Jay Z was Blake's all-time favorite rapper, but music did not factor into their conversation. Instead they spoke of sports team investments and other

business. Blake revealed that he and Alexus had at one time planned to purchase a large slice of the Chicago Bulls franchise.

Beyoncé said she would be sending over a track she wanted Bulletface to feature on, and he promised to record his verse as soon as he got it.

Kim told Blake that her sister Khloe had a huge crush on him; he gave her his number to give to Khloe.

An editor for Rolling Stone magazine who happened to be in the VIP section spoke to Blake about possibly being on an upcoming cover.

Smartphone cameras flashed nonstop as people snapped pictures of the celebs in VIP. Draya ended up sitting next to Blake when he made it back to his table; Nona and Barbie seemed to catch attitudes about it, but neither of them spoke on it.

Then Draya whispered something in Blake's ear that had him ready to leave right then.

"With all this money you're throwing around, I bet your bedroom must look fly as fuck. When you gon' let me see it?"

"Shit, whenever you wanna see that muhfucka," he replied with an honest chuckle.

"Yeah? So it's me and you tonight?" Draya was persistent. She had a cocktail glass in hand with some crazy concoction of liquor in it, and she was nursing it through a straw.

Blake nodded, raising his double-stacked Styrofoam cups to take a drink of Lean...and suddenly he found himself face to face with Barbie.

She was standing off to the side of his table, hands on her hips, eyes squinted, nostrils flaring— fuming.

"You got Tasia Olsen more fucked up than you could possibly even know right now," Barbie said.

Blake laughed and stood up.

"We need to talk," Barbie said. "Now."

"Look, you ain't my girlfriend. Don't start that trippin' shit. I just met you a couple days ago."

"Negro, please. I wanna go home. Now." A conspiratorial smirk appeared on her perfect face. "And if you don't wanna take me home it's cool." She glanced toward Chris Brown's table. "Chris said he'll take me. His guys just pulled up. We got a ride."

"I ain't doin' noooo trippin'." Blake sipped some more Lean as the reality of what he'd gotten himself into struck him.

He remembered hearing somewhere that Draya and Chris had once dated for a while.

Now that Draya was all up in his face, Barbie was feeling some type of way, and she knew the perfect man to leave with that would upset Draya at the same time.

Or maybe he was thinking too much.

Whatever the case, he liked Draya a lot— always had ever since he saw her on The Real Basketball Wives of LA teaching Gloria how to pole dance

— and he didn't care how the night ended, as long as he got himself some of Draya.

In the infamous words of Chris Brown himself, Blake chucked up the deuces to Barbie and watched the dime piece shrug her shoulders and saunter over to Chris's table.

The party went on for another half hour before Chris and his guys left. Boosie left with Jeezy and YG.

Kevin Gates' girlfriend Dreka had joined them in VIP minutes earlier; the two of them departed together shortly before Hove, Queen Bey, Yeezy, and Kim left.

Bulletface and his entourage were essentially the last to leave.

As they were exiting the massive club, Blake noticed that Bubbles had also gone missing. He asked Meach if he'd seen her.

"She snuck off wit' Jeezy n'em, bruh," Meach said. Blake could only laugh.

He realized then that no matter how much money a person had, women would be women and men would be men. In the land of millionaires, women bounced from bed to bed just like they did in the hood. The only thing different was the thread count.

He didn't mind, though.

After all, he had the women he wanted for the night, and he was pretty sure he knew what they wanted.

He had a duffle bag full of it.

Chapter 21

The headlights on Charlie Mack's red Bentley coupe came on just as the Bulletface tour bus was pulling away from the curb outside Avalon

Hollywood.

There was a swamp green Toyota parked behind him; its engine started when his did, and together they slowly began driving up the densely packed street.

"That's that nigga right there," Mack said into his smartphone. "Just follow me, a'ight, Blood? When I say let go, let that mothafucka go! You hear me?"

He was talking to Tyrone Stalling, Jacob's 17-year-old brother, who was the passenger in the Toyota.

"I ain't wit' all this chitchat, Mack. They killed my brother. Just tell me when and I'm gon' flip that whole fuckin' bus over."

Tyrone's voice was full of emotion. Hatred, anger, and a host of other dangerous emotions that would guarantee zero hesitation when it came time to pull the trigger.

Mack smiled. He liked being in charge, was used to it, in fact. He had a bunch of young Bloods on his payroll and hundreds more fighting to take their spots. His plan to make a little extra change off the rap star's chain hadn't fallen through, but there was still a chance of extortion. He could have the tour bus riddled with bullets, and if the billionaire survived, he could step in like the OG he was and make some demands. $100,000 seemed reasonable, but who knew how much he could ultimately get.

Charles Mack was considered a millionaire in Compton (or Bompton, as his Bloods always called it), but in all actuality he wasn't doing quite that well.

The Bentley was a rental from a car dealership the father of an ex- girlfriend of his owned, and he was five months behind on payments.

He had a nice quarter-million-dollar minimansion in West Hollywood, but the $2,200-a-month mortgage was treating a hole in his savings, which had dwindled down to just under $100,000 over the past year.

Last summer, a federal drug sweep in Compton had cost Mack twelve kilos of heroin, seventeen kilos of coke, and over $300,000 in cash. Not to mention all the workers he'd lost in the raids.

He hadn't been able to bounce back ever since.

He had owed $200,000 to his drug connect — a Mexican Mafia member he'd met in Soledad prison twenty years ago— but he'd wired up on old Chavez for the feds and gotten rid of that problem. The Mexican Mafia had a bounty on his head but he didn't care. He had too many soldiers in

Compton, and he rarely left their presence without having at least one car full of the young gunslingers close by for security.

He'd recently found a new connect in Arizona with kilos of coke for

$22,000 apiece, and he was making $70,000 off every kilo, slowly climbing his way back up to kingpin status.

With the help of Jake's grieving brother, he hoped to make that climb just a little easier.

The tour bus turned off Vine Street and onto Hollywood Boulevard.

Mack was five car-lengths behind, cruising slow and purposefully, waiting on the perfect opportunity to speed up beside the tour bus with his shooter ready to open fire.

There were too many witnesses now. Too many cars, too many blacked out SUVs that could be police for all Mack knew.

One of those blacked out SUVs was tailing the long black tour bus. Mack hoped it wasn't police.

Tyrone must have read his mind.

"What's up with that black Escalade, Mack? Think it's his security or some shit?"

"I don't know and I don't give a fuck. That nigga had his bodyguards kill lil Blood. They choked him to death, lil Ty! He gon' pay for that!"

"I'm ready to do this shit now. Fuck waitin'."

"Give it a second. Let the crowd clear out. I'm tryna get closer."

Mack attempted to swerve around the black Ford sedan in front of him but the driver swerved over to stop him.

He laughed.

"God's on your side, Bulletface," he cackled, gently stroking his goatee. "Better hope he sticks with you."

He tried the swerve again a moment later and got the same result. The Ford swerved with him.

He gritted his teeth and pounded the steering wheel, then opened the glovebox and grabbed his .357 Magnum.

"Swerve again, mothafucka," he snarled. "I dare you."

King Rio

Chapter 22

"I swear on my mother's grave, Pedro, if you drop some spikes on somebody else tonight, or kill somebody else tonight, you'll never hear from me again."

Pedro looked in Mary's sweet brown eyes and saw nothing but fear. She was obviously growing tired of the daily cartel drama, and by the looks of it, the drama was not yet over.

She had on a black dress now, with yellow bolts of lightening down the sides. Her hair was still impeccable. Her face was just as hypnotically attractive as it was when Pedro first saw her in Mexico.

Following the Bulletface concert, the four of them— Pedro, Sergio, Lisa, and Mary— had gone to The Egyptian Theatre on Hollywood Boulevard for a screening of "Mad Summer". There they'd shared chocolate covered raisins and popcorn and whispered about a number of things, hardly watching the film at all but enjoying it nonetheless.

Pedro had learned that Lisa's mother was actually an old schoolmate of his, and that Mary was allergic to seafood, hated the movie "Shawshank Redemption", disliked sports, and loved Netflix.

Then, in the middle of the movie, he'd received a call from the team of men he had watching over Blake saying the MBM guys were getting ready to leave Avalon Hollywood, which happened to be just around the corner from The Egyptian Theatre.

He'd rushed everyone out to his rented Escalade and raced to Avalon, knowing that, after the Staples Center incident, Blake's name would be on fire.

Now he was in the back of the Escalade with Lisa and Mary. Sergio was driving, and he was directly behind the Bulletface tour bus.

Mary had good reason to be worried.

The miniature AK-47 was on Pedro's lap again.

It wasn't the same one from the Chicago shooting; that one was somewhere in Lake Michigan.

No, this one was brand-new, with a 50-round banana clip and red laser sighting.

"Settle down," Pedro said to Mary as he studied the camera monitor. He and his men were watching the Bentley and the Toyota following it. Two of his men in a Ford Fusion three cars back had already cut off the
Bentley twice.

"Don't you fucking dare!" Mary said.

But it was too late.

Pedro's men knew that something was up, and they were ready to make their move.

An earpiece was keeping Pedro on tune with his two men in the Ford. "They're trying to get around us, Pedro. He's tried twice already. The guy
in the Bentley."

After a moment of thought, Pedro said, "Hit him. Hit the bastard. Crash into him right goddamn now!"

"No!" Mary said.

Lisa's eyes got wide but she didn't utter a single word. There was a screech and a loud crash.

Pedro looked back and saw that smoke was rising from the hood of the Bentley. The driver's door swung open and out stepped a heavyset man wearing an all red suit.

"He's armed! And the Toyota's coming around!"

"Shit. Shoot him," Pedro said into his earpiece. Then he told Sergio to cut off the Toyota before it could reach the tour bus.

Mary and Lisa dove to the floor just as the Escalade made a sharp left turn in the middle of traffic.

Gunshots rang out.

Pedro rolled his window down just before the Toyota collided with the Escalade's driver's door.

Two men got out of the Toyota with red bandanas tied around the lower halves of their faces and pistols with extended clips in their hands.

One of them aimed at the tour bus while the other looked back to see where the gunshots had come from behind them.

Pedro pushed open his door took aim at the man who had the tour bus in his sights just as the man started shooting. He only got off two shots before Pedro filled his back with holes.

As Pedro turned to take aim at the second thug, a bullet

114

pierced his suit jacket and knocked him against his open door. Another round hit his chest, then another, and another, before he was finally able to lift the AK-47 and drill the second gunman to the ground.

King Rio

Chapter 23

Frightened by the sudden explosions of gunfire, Draya ran off the bus in the middle of Sunset Boulevard.

Blake didn't know whether to duck or run outside and return fire. He and everyone else on the bus ducked low. He pulled the gun from out of his duffle bag, while Biggs took ahold of the AK-47 Blake had left on the table before entering Avalon.

His driver stomped on the gas. The tour bus lurched forward.

"Bruh, you good?" Scrill asked Blake.

Blake nodded and glanced over to check on Nona. Her brother, Biggs, was lying over her, shielding her with his body.

"Kendall!" Blake shouted.

"I'm fine, I'm fine!" Kendall replied. She was in the bathroom with the door shut.

The chauffeur made a series of turns that took them right back past Avalon Hollywood. Remo didn't know which way to go, he was just trying to flee the shooting.

"What the fuck was that about, bruh?" Biggs said a moment later, when all the guys were back on heir feet with their guns in hand.

"Fuck if I know." Blake went to the wide window on the driver's side of the tour bus and gazed out. He laughed at his luck. "Is it me, or do we attract gunshots everywhere we go? Damn. Every fuckin' city it's the same shit. Drill season."

"It's that nigga Chief Keef's fault," Meach said with a nervous laugh as he joined Blake at the window. "Got everybody wantin' to bang bang and shit."

They all shared a laugh. Blake's phone started ringing. It was Bubbles calling.

"I know you saw what just went down," she said when he answered. "It's three dead bodies out here on Sunset. They was coming at either you or somebody else on that tour bus. I'm sitting here in the car with a girl I don't even know. We was a couple cars behind the red Bentley that crashed.

That's what started the whole beef, I think. Why the fuck did you leave me at the club?"

"Bruh said you left with Jeezy."

"Boy, please, I talked to that nigga and went to the bathroom. When I came out you was gone. Got me sitting here in this lady's car. Where y'all at?"

They all shared another laugh as Remo pulled over and waited for Bubbles. She arrived in a white Buick with a young white girl Blake remembered seeing inside the club. He got out, took a picture with the woman, and gave her $500 for the trouble. She said she couldn't believe she'd just taken a picture with Bulletface and that all her Facebook and Instagram friends were going to be so jealous.

"You made that girl's day," Bubbles said as they rejoined the gang on the bus. She looked around, using an index finger to count every person. "Where'd ya lil girlfriend go?"

"Haaaaa," Meach said. "She heard gunshots and jumped ship."

Blake shook his head and took a seat at the table. Scrill poured up some Sprite and Codeine. Meach rolled two fat blunts. Bubbles sat her phat ass on Blake's lap, and he got happy about it, though he didn't say it.

Everyone — even Kendall and Remo — smoked the blunts. Soon more were being rolled and passed around.

By the time they made it back to the mansion, an ounce of Kush had been smoked. Blake carried his duffle bag into the kitchen, where his personal chefs were already busy whipping up steak tacos and a host of other goodies for the king of the castle.

Kendall had called ahead to get them started cooking.

The scrumptious scent of frying steak made Blake's mouth water. He absolutely could not take it. He signaled for Nona and Bubbles to follow him and then led the way to his master bedroom.

He fell back on the bed and kicked his shoes off. "I'm so high and tired," he said with his eyes shut.

"You ain't the only one." Nona fell next to him. "I shouldn't have been drinking so much in VIP. Shit got me out of it."

Blake sat up and slapped Nona on the ass. Bubbles was simultaneously lifting her dress over her head and kicking off her heels in the bathroom doorway. She got in the tub minutes later, and Blake took a shower. Then Nona got up and ran herself some bath water while Blake lay on the bed with Bubbles mounted on him.

"Your bodyguards killed that boy," Bubbles said, rubbing her

118

hands over his bulging pectoral muscles. "That's crazy as hell. He was wrong for snatching your necklace but he didn't deserve to die about it, you know what I'm sayin'? That's so messed up."

"Fuck that nigga." Blake's hands roamed freely over the meaty buttocks that Bubbles possessed. She had on a black lace bra and panties set, and all he wore was a pair of black and gold Versace boxers and his diamond jewelry.

For the first time, Blake noticed that the bit of gut she'd once had was gone.

"You been exercising?" he asked.

She shook her head no. "Remember that $500,000 you gave me and Shay that day in Chicago? I went and got a tummy tuck. It's sad it took you this damn long to notice."

"I don't be looking at no stomachs. I ain't tryna fuck no stomachs, so what the fuck I'ma look at em for?"

She gave him a soft slap to the cheek. "Asshole."

"Now that, I'll fuck." He grinned his grin and poked out his lips for a kiss. "I can't stand your black ass." Bubbles laughed. She didn't kiss him.

Instead she went all thoughtful on him. "Do you know how much money you've given me over the years? Since that shit with the nigga Jazzy in Gary?"

"A whole lot."

"Yeah. I know. I saved most of it, you know that? I never went crazy spending the way you do. I got my baby Ra'Mya's college tuition all paid up and she's only seven years old. I own my houses in Chicago and New York, and the one in New York is being rented out for $1,600-a-month. I have a lot of money in the bank. Don't even have to work. You made sure I was set for life. I can never thank you enough."

"Yes, you can." Blake gave a suggestive grin, then laughed it off. "That shit ain't nothin'. If I could go back in time I'd probably give you even more. I'm like that. Love to see people doing good."

"You're a great man, Blake. I just wanted to tell you that. I know folks that would kill to have a friend like you. My mom still can't believe how blessed I've been messing around with you. She says it's God's work, but I don't know about all that."

She let out a soft laugh.

Blake reached over to the nightstand for the remote control and turned on the television, an 80-inch smart TV. He went straight to MTN News, which was owned by Costilla Corp., Alexus's corporation.

The breaking news was all about Bulletface.

Bubbles watched through the headboard mirror's reflection.

'...A shooting on the Sunset strip involving rapper Bulletface and his entourage has resulted in the deaths of three alleged Compton gang members, one of whom was a federal informant. We're also receiving reports that one of the deceased may be somehow related to the man who was killed outside the Staples Center following an incident where he attempted to steal Bullet-face's necklace during an onstage performance. The rapper's bodyguards are participating with investigators, according to the LAPD. They're saying the victim, Jacob Stalling, was violently resisting as he was being escorted out of the Staples Center, and he died as bodyguards were trying to restrain him. The Sunset Boulevard shooting is reportedly being investigated as a retaliatory attempt by the Compton gang Stalling was affiliated with.

'Bulletface is now wanted for questioning in both the shooting investigation and Jacob Stalling's death...'

"Bullshit," Blake said with a chuckle.

"You need to calm your ass down, Blake. For real." Bubbles sounded serious. She gave him a second soft slap to the face, then a third. "Don't be a fool. You're too rich for all that mess."

"I didn't do shit but knock a nigga out for snatchin' my chain. Anybody would've did that."

"Yeah, but your bodyguards killed the guy. And now three people are laying dead out there on Sunset because of it."

Blake shrugged. "I just wanna know how the niggas got killed on Sunset.

I know me and my niggas didn't shoot nobody." "Cops might've seen em."

"They didn't say nothin' 'bout no cops. And I didn't see no cops."

"Some people were following the tour bus. I saw that. I saw a few of them get out of a car with machine guns aimed at the dude from the Bentley, but that's all I saw until the shooting stopped 'cause me and the white girl ducked down until it was over."

Blake's hands traveled along Bubbles' thighs as he pondered over the incident.

His dick became hard; the warmth of her pussy was getting to him.

He came to the conclusion that either Pedro or another Costilla Cartel member was behind the Sunset Boulevard shooting.

If that was the case, the cartel was following him.

"It was Pedro tryna save my life again," he said. "I know it."

Bubbles grinded on him. He squeezed and smacked his hands onto her ass again, but this time instead of moving them he squeezed and pulled downward, biting the center of his lower lip.

"You gon' make me forget all about that, huh?" he murmured. She nodded. "That's what I intend to do."

"Show me," Blake encouraged.

She regarded him with the kind of innocent look a woman gives a man just before she puts it on him.

Her hands went inside his boxers as she moved back and freed his erection. She gawked at it, as if she'd never seen it before, and she began pumping it in her hands.

"I'm literally surprised every time I see this thing," Bubbles said as she went to all fours. She licked her lips and kissed the underside of it. "It's so fucking big. Shit. I don't know how it just fits inside me like that. It looks too big."

Blake's grin brightened. He interlaced his fingers behind his head and watched the thick redbone's mouth open to take in his fat phallus.

Her mouth did a slow suck-lip-slurp dance on the head of his dick while she gripped, pumped, and twisted his length in her hands.

"Sixty-nine that shit," he said. "Let me taste that pussy."

She did not hesitate to turn so that her delicious-smelling pussy was hovering right over his mouth.

At first he licked and sucked her through the panties, inhaling through his nose the wonderful scent of her juicy nookie. Then he moved them to the side and got the full meal, sucking and tonguing her clitoris, delving his tongue deep inside her as she sucked him to the rear of her throat again and again.

Just then, Nona came walking out if the bathroom. She was in a white robe, holding her hips and watching the x-rated show.

"That's what I'm talkin' about, Bubbles. Suck the skin off that dick," Nona said in a lascivious whisper. She opened the robe and pushed her boobs together, then inserted a finger in her pussy and stroked herself to a cotton- soft moan.

The news was still on. Now they were discussing something between Mariah Carey and Nick Cannon. It all went in one ear and out the other.

Bubbles tasted better than Thanksgiving dinner, and Blake never wanted to stop licking her.

A couple of minutes passed before Nona joined in. Bubbles sat up on Blake's mouth, bouncing and wiggling on his tongue. She let Nona do the sucking, which Nona did quite well.

Several times Blake had to lift Bubbles up to catch a breath, but every time he went back to sucking on her wet nookie and enjoying the sounds of her moans.

He heard Nona gag and choke a couple of times as she sucked him. Then she mounted him and guided his stiff pole inside her and rode him wildly, slamming down on him with every downward bounce. The wet sucking sound her sex made was like nitro to Blake's veins, compelling him to thrust up to go in as deep as his foot-long pole could possibly go.

Bubbles tensed up on his mouth; his tongue was going a mile a minute on her clit, and she could no longer take it.

He slowed to a steady licking all across her pussy as she shook and trembled in orgasm. Then she moved off of him and lay panting beside him as Nona rode him until she too was trembling from the big O and collapsing onto the bed.

Blake got up on his knees, moving his hips so that his glistening-wet pole swung from side to side.

"I ain't done, what the fuck y'all doin'?"

Nona and Bubbles laughed joyously, knowing that neither of them were off the hook.

They would need to have a lot more stamina to last with Blake King. He was ready to go all night.

Chapter 24

"This is the second time we've had to switch out of shot-up cars today," Sergio pointed out.

Pedro rudely rolled up the partition on Sergio, cutting the driver off from him and the girls.

They were in an armored black Mercedes Maybach limousine now, one similar to the vehicles most celebs in Hollywood used when they were in fear of their lives from the occasional stalker.

Trailing behind them were three regular-sized black Maybachs that were also armored. The men occupying them were heavily armed, ex-military Costilla Cartel soldiers in expensive black business suits.

Sitting across from Pedro, Mary and Lisa were dressed like A-list actresses in flowing Valentino gowns. Diamonds shined brightly on their wrists and necks. Following the Sunset shooting, Pedro had hired the best stylists in all of Hollywood to dress the ladies in this season's hottest fashions, since it was supposed to be their last evening together.

Pedro himself had changed into a white Gucci suit and tie with a simple gold Rolex watch added to upgrade his look just a tad bit more than it already was. He'd given the girls more money to split between the two of them, $50,000 this time.

The bulletproof vest he'd worn earlier was resting on Mary's lap. She was examining it in awe.

"You are so fucking lucky," she murmured, unable to take her eyes off the bullets that were stuck in the vest. "This is insane. I mean insanely insane."

"Yeah," Lisa said, "and these dresses and diamonds are insanely expensive. You should let us keep it all to go home with."

Pedro lifted a shoulder in a half shrug and looked out his window.

The procession of Maybachs were heading up a long, winding hill to the mansion where he knew that Blake was staying the night.

"Why are all those Maybachs following us?" Mary asked. "Jesus, I feel like I'm in that movie "Coming To America". This all seems like a dream."

"It is a dream," Pedro said. "It's the American dream. It's the lifestyle that every single person in this country dreams of one day living, am I right?

And I'm giving it all to you free of charge."

Mary shook her head. "Nothing's free in this world. You want something out of this. I just haven't figured out what yet."

"What if I just want someone to see that none of it means anything without...I don't know. Never mind."

"No. Continue. Please."

Pedro shook his head no. "I'll sound like Shakespeare." He laughed and played with his tie. "It's nothing. Really."

"Well," Mary said, tossing the vest to him, "if there's some romantic point to this, I'm more than interested in hearing it. Did that drink at the bar leave you feeling like you needed to take some Black girl out of the ghetto and show her the rich side of life? Is that it? Because if it is I'm lost as to why

you'd want to do such a thing. I'll still be the same girl from a poor Indianapolis family like I was when we first met. I'll still be —"

"Stop it, will you?"

"No. I'm being honest. Sorry if you can't handle the truth, Mr. Richie Fucking Rich. Thanks for the money, had a great, dangerous time with you, thanks a lot for that. Now take us to LAX and get me and my friend on a plane to El Paso."

A deafening silence ensued. Mary's expression was suddenly one of anger; even Lisa seemed stunned by it.

The fleet of Maybachs were just turning into the circular driveway in front of Blake's massive hilltop mansion.

"Fine," Pedro said finally. "Let me talk to Blake, and then we'll go straight to the airport. My deepest apologies for the inconvenience."

Sergio parked the limo, and Pedro got out immediately. His emotions were bothering him.

He didn't like emotions.

"What was I thinking?" he muttered under his breath.

His only answer to the damning question was that he might have chosen to take the girl on a trip because he was genuinely attracted to her. She was a cute-faced college girl with her entire life ahead of her, not some wannabe Griselda Blanco like most of the women who ran in his circle.

But of course he knew that was BS.

He'd met hundreds of women over his thirty years of living and not once had he ever taken a liking to a woman the way he had with Mary. He'd spent money on women, but only after sleeping with them, and whenever he grew tired of the sex he ended the relationships completely. No strings attached was his specialty.

With Mary, however, there had been something more. That's what he'd felt, at least.

Damn those emotions.

Shaking away the troublesome thoughts, Pedro rang the door-bell and flamed up a cigar while he waited, turning to look back at the limousine where the stunning young Black woman was waiting to make her return home to El Paso.

The tall oak door swung open and a curvaceous white woman stepped out.

Pedro recognized her as Blake's personal assistant. "Oh," she yelped in surprise. "Pedro."

"I need a word with Blake."

"He's, um...busy at the moment. Would you mind coming back tomorrow?"

"It can't wait. Urgent message."

"Well, he's asleep, so there's really nothing I can —"

"Tell him it's me. He's waiting on me. And don't you dare shut this for in my face. Now go."

Reluctantly, the curvy white girl turned and stormed off through the foyer.

She'd made a wise decision. Pedro didn't want to hurt her. Not in front of Mary. The girl had seen more deaths in a single day than most people saw in a lifetime.

Things were about to get a lot more deadly in the coming hours. Which is why Pedro was here to warn Blake.

King Rio

Chapter 25

"I knew this was gon' get both of y'all geeked up," Blake said, his tone replete with arrogance.

Nona and Bubbles were kneeled down on the bed with their faces down and their asses up, sucking and licking each other's lips as Blake King made it rain hundreds on their backs while thrusting his rigid pole into Bubbles' slippery pussy.

He'd been sleepy when they first arrived at the mansion; now he was wide awake. For the moment, at least.

There came a knock at the bedroom door. "Blake." It was Kendall. "You've got company." "I'm busy," he replied quickly.

"I assumed that."

"Tell em to come back tomorrow."

"I did. It's Pedro Costilla. He's not leaving. Says it's urgent."

Blake kept right on plowing Bubbles. He was biting the middle of his lower lip again. His scrotum was tingling in anticipation of an imminent eruption.

He pulled out of her and slipped into Nona and continued to thrust with reckless abandon.

"Are you coming or not?" Kendall asked.

"Yeah, I'm coming," he said, yanking out and letting his semen rocket forward over Bubbles and Nona's roiling derrières. "In more ways than one," he added with a chuckle, halfway out of breath.

He slapped his deflating phallus on Nona's ass until the last drops of semen were out and then took the robe she'd worn out of the bathroom and put it and his boxers on.

His duffle bag was open at the foot of his bed. He'd taken $20,000 out of it to throw on the girls. He picked up the duffle with one hand and took his gun out of it with the other.

"I'll be right back," he said, using his forearm to swipe beads of sweat from his hairline.

He opened the door and found Kendall standing there with a huge smile on her face.

"Big guy," she said with a knowing smirk.

He breezed past her and headed up the hallway. She walked with him. Instinctively, he cocked the slide back on the pistol, chambering a round.

There was never any telling if things would go safely when the Costilla Cartel was involved.

"Where the fuck my niggas at?" he asked.

"They're out in the swimming pool. They had some women they met at the concert come over."

The swimming pool was behind the mansion.

"I'ma need to start hiring some muhfuckin security around this bitch," Blake said.

"You've got enough in that duffle bag to hire a full-time security team." "Don't worry about what I got in my duffle bag." He gave her a stern look.

"I pay you, don't I? Ain't that enough?"

Kendall didn't respond. She continued on with him to the front door. He paused when he made it to the door.

The look on Pedro's face was worth a thousand words.

"Gamuza," Pedro said, toking on a fat cigar. "He has a twenty-million- dollar bounty on you and your family."

Blake looked past Pedro at the fleet of Maybachs. "My family?"

Pedro nodded. "Yes. You, your brother, and both of your children. He knows you're running the Costilla family business while Alexus is in the coma. He wants you all dead."

"But...I thought he was with us?"

"He was." Another nod from Pedro. "Not anymore, though."

"What changed?"

"What changed is Alexus is in a coma. She's at least half Mexican. You're a Black guy, a fucking rap star, for Christ's sake. He's embarrassed to be under your rule. El Chapo's been laughing at us from his prison cell, and the Sinaloas who aren't with us have been digging a tunnel to free him. Gamuza thinks El Chapo will come home and take over Mexico if things continue the way they're going now...with you in charge."

Blake gritted his teeth. "Fuck Gamuza. Didn't he kill Alexus's grandaddy?

We should've offed his old ass a long time ago." "Yeah, but we didn't. Now he's after you."

It was Blake's turn to nod. "A'ight. Bet that up. Send some people to kill him first."

"If only it were that simple." Pedro turned his back to Blake. Suddenly he was staring at the Maybach limo that was parked near the Bulletface tour bus. "You see, we have no idea where he's located. He's practically invisible, therefore he's invincible until we know of his whereabouts. You, on the other hand, are an international celebrity. It's much easier for him to find you than it is for us to find him."

Blake became thoughtful: he clenched his teeth tightly together and flared his nostrils, holding his gun in a death-grip.

He'd already lost his parents to the cartel lifestyle; he wasn't about to lose his children.

"Want my advice?" Pedro asked. "Nah," Blake said sarcastically.

"I say you lay low somewhere and let me handle this. I've been dealing with these guys for years. Let me get to him before he gets to you. Take your kids and take a flight to the other side of the world if you need to. I promise, I'll have all this squared away in no time."

It took Blake a long moment to reply. When he did, his hand was locked so tightly around the pistol that he feared he'd accidentally pull the trigger if he didn't pay attention to it.

"I'm gon' cut that old bitch's head off like he did Segovia Costilla. Watch.

I got him."

"No," Pedro said. "I'll handle it. Just do me a favor and get this fine woman of mine and her friend home to El Paso, Texas. I'll tend to the dirty work."

Blake gave a half nod.

Pedro turned to leave. "I'll follow you to LAX," he said. "Hurry up. We haven't got all day."

King Rio

Chapter 26

Two black vans full of Zeta Cartel militants who'd ventured across the border from Mexico through a drug tunnel were racing up the hill toward Blake "Bulletface" King's hilltop mansion at that very minute.

The men in the rear of the minivans were all watching a recording their boss, Gamuza, had left for them on two Samsung computer tablets.

"You have all been trained for times like this," Gamuza began. "Tonight I ask of you the deepest, most meaningful of favors, not only for me and our fellow men but also for the future of our country.

"An imposter has been bestowed the blessing of running OUR drug operations. This is something that cannot and must not go on. You are to locate Blake King and any of his descendants and do to them what we've done to impostors in Mexico since the beginning of time.

"Kill and behead them!"

The men understood their orders perfectly.

King Rio

Chapter 27

"Everybody get dressed! Right the fuck now! We gotta go! Meet me out front!"

Blake's voice echoed all throughout the mansion.

He was holding down the button on the intercom next to his bedroom door as he yanked on a pair of white Balmain jeans and stepped into his pearl white Louboutin sneakers.

Nona and Bubbles were dressing hurriedly. "What's going on?" Nona asked.

"Don't worry about it. Just get dressed. Hurry up."

He strapped on his bulletproof vest and went to his walk-in closet to get his AR-15 assault rifle. Heart racing, he threw the shoulder-strap over his neck and returned to the bedroom, eyes flicking about frantically. Kendall was in the bedroom doorway, looking like she didn't have a clue what was going on.

When the girls were dressed, they headed out together, with Blake in front like some heroic character in an action movie.

Only this was real life.

If a soul was lost, there would be no coming back in another role.

When they made it to the foyer, Biggs, Meach, Will Scrill, and their lady friends were standing there with Remo, all of them looking confused.

But not too confused to not have their guns drawn and at the ready.

Every MBM recording artist held a semiautomatic pistol with a 30-round clip.

"Let's go," Blake said urgently. "We gotta go right—"

His words were cut short by the sudden explosions of fully automatic gunfire.

King Rio

Chapter 28

Mary gasped at the sound of gunshots.

Pedro was just climbing back into the limo. He froze and picked up the miniature AK-47 from in front of his seat just as a van with its sliding doors open came veering into the circular drive.

Assault rifles were belching fire from within the open sliding doors. "Jesus!" Lisa shrieked as she and Mary slid down in their seats.

Pedro's cartel soldiers got out of the Maybachs and returned fire. Bullet after bullet pinged into the limousine's armored exterior.

"What the fuck, Pedro?!" Mary said. "Do something! Get us away from here!"

But Pedro was momentarily frozen in place. He stared out his window at the blazing guns, unsure of what he should do.

Sergio lowered the privacy glass partition. "Want me to drive through these fucks?"

Pedro shook his head no. "We can't leave Blake."

"Forget about Blake! These men are here to kill, and I'm not gonna be a fucking murder victim!"

Sergio stomped on the gas pedal; the limo's tires churned and screeched as it began to speed off.

Swiftly, Pedro turned and put the AK-47's barrel to the back of Sergio's head. "We are not leaving without Blake. Simple as that."

The limousine stopped moving just as suddenly as it had started. Almost instantly, nine bullets stitched across the windshield.

The gunfire was deafening.

Pedro looked to the mansion's front door just as the lawn lights went off. Blake and half a dozen others came running outside. They all were heading for the tour bus. Blake and his guys were shooting their guns as they ran.

There were three of Pedro's men on the ground wounded already. A couple of the enemy's men were also grounded.

Pedro lowered his window just enough to stick the assault rifle barrel out and sent multiple rounds at a masked gunman who was firing in Blake's direction.

He hit the gunman high in the chest and again in the throat, knocking him into the van's open sliding door.

The steady boom of gunfire became less and less frequent as more and more gunmen were subtracted from both sides. Seconds seemed like hours.

Pedro continued to squeeze off shots from over his window. He took down two more men before the Bulletface tour bus went crashing past a van.

"Follow behind them!" Pedro shouted to Sergio.

He kept shooting as the limo went speeding off down the hill behind the tour bus.

Out of the corner of his eye, he saw Mary crouched down in front of her seat with her knees to her chest and her hands on her head.

Lisa's arms were wrapped tight around Mary's shoulders. "We're gonna be okay," Lisa kept saying.

Pedro wondered if Lisa's statement would ultimately ring true.

Chapter 29

"I'm shot! I'm shot! Oh, my God, I'm shot!" Remo screamed out in pain. "Just keep drivin', nigga! That lil shit ain't nothin'!" Blake was at the front

of the tour bus with his driver, Remo, looking at the gushing bullet wound in the old guy's left shoulder.

"I'll drive," Nona said.

The tour bus swerved from left to right as she maneuvered into the driver's seat over Remo. He fell off to the side, eyes wide, pressing a palm to the gaping hole.

Blake dragged Remo to the rear of the Newell coach bus. Kendall found a first aid kit.

Gunshots were still clapping in the distance.

"What have you gotten us into, Blake?!" Bubbles said.

Blake looked at the gun in his hand. Smoke was drifting up into the air from its barrel.

He shifted his eyes to the guys, all of whom were standing alert with their own smoking guns in hand.

Worried that Rita and the kids could be going through a similar situation, he dialed Rita's cell phone and waited anxiously through five eternally long rings.

"Hey, stranger," Rita answered. "What, are you calling for another thirty minute outing with the kids? Because they're already asleep."

Blake blew a sigh of relief. "Y'all gotta get outta there, Ma. I'm talking asap. Right this minute."

"Get out of here? Why? I don't plan on leaving California until my baby is out of that hospital."

"Nah, Ma. It's serious. You gotta take the kids and leave. Some people just came after me. They'll be looking for the kids too."

"We've got security, Blake. There are twenty-five asked men out there. I'll call in more if need be, but I'm not waking up my grandbabies at this time of night to go running because of that stuff that happened on Sunset. Yes, I saw it all on the news. We're safe here. If anything it's you who needs to pack up and leave."

Blake gritted his teeth in frustration. "I'm coming to get my kids." "That's fine by me. I'll be here waiting. Call when you get here."

Blake's iPhone rang the second the call with Rita ended. This time it was Pedro.

"I just lost eight men. It's a massacre back there," Pedro said. "Get out of here, alright. I'll go to Mexico and end this nonsense. Just get on your plane and go."

Suddenly Blake was angry with the Costilla Cartel itself. "This shit ain't what's up. Fuck this whole cartel business. I'm done with all this shit. You can take over if you —"

"You can't just step down, Blake." "Yes the fuck I can!"

"You're married to Alexus Costilla. She's the cocaine queen, you know what I mean? Whether you like it or not, you're in this game for the long run."

Blake couldn't stop grinding his teeth together. He was red-hot. The MBM gang looked just as upset.

"A'ight, I'm taking a break from all this shit out here, though. I'm canceling all my shows until Alexus is back, and I'm laying low until then too. One."

He hit 'end' and dropped the phone on his lap. Looking around, he noticed that all eyes were on him. "So," Biggs asked. "What's the thought?"

"Y'all go on and finish the tour." Blake kept his eyes on the bullet holes in the bus's side windows. "I'm done with this shit for now. Got a son I ain't never even met. I'm picking him up and taking my kids to Spain for the next few weeks. Barcelona, Spain. Fuck it. I gotta get the fuck away from all this gunplay."

Chapter 30

Tonight it was Aretha Franklin that soothed Rita to sleep; and it was a single gunshot that awakened her.

She sat up in bed, eyes flicking every which way. The clock read 11:47 pm.

Vari and King Neal came running into the room and leapt up onto the bed with Rita.

"Grandma, did you hear that?" Vari asked.

"Sit here with your brother." Rita got up and went to her dresser. She tugged open her to drawer and reached way to the back, underneath a neatly folded sweatshirt, and withdrew a Tec-9 submachine gun.

She'd gone to the shooting range for more than seven weeks in a row two years ago, perfecting her aim for occasions like this.

"Oooooh," King said, pointing at the fully-automatic weapon. "Look what Grandma got." His eyes were as wide as saucers.

Slowly, quietly, Rita tiptoed to the door and pushed it shut. Her history with the Costilla Cartel had been a key factor in her decision to have a deadbolt lock installed on her door. She twisted it and sighed when it thumped into the locking mechanism.

Then came two more thunderous gunshots. Vari snatched her brother into her arms.

Rita rushed to the television, turned it on, and went to the camera monitors just as the phone on her nightstand started ringing.

Her mouth fell open at what she saw on the television.

All around the mansion, sprawled out disproportionately on the rolling green lawns, on the tennis court, and in the driveway, were the men and women that made up her security team.

Neither of them were moving. Horrified, she picked up the phone.

"I'm outside your bedroom door." It was Enrique, the man who'd been the head of Alexus's personal bodyguard and the chief of her security team for several years now. "They've got snipers out there, took out our guys in the blink of an eye, but I don't think there's many of them. I just got three of them. Sit tight, okay? If someone comes to this door and doesn't call your phone first, give them all you've got. I'll be back when I know it's safe."

Rita's hands were trembling as she hung up the phone.

"What's going on, Grandma?" Vari asked with tears in her eyes. "Yeah, Grandma," King added.

There was a Holy Bible on the nightstand. Rita set the gun down and picked up the good book.

"Everything's fine," she said as she joined her grandchildren in bed. "Let's see what message God has for us tonight."

King started crying. "I want my daddy!"

Chapter 31

The tingling sensation that had accompanied the loss of Enrique's left hand was a bit irritating, but the new prosthetic steel hand worked better than his right hand did. In the prosthetic hand he held an iPad that showed views from the mansion's interior and exterior cameras. In the other hand he held a Glock pistol with an extended magazine and green laser sighting.

He'd used the iPad to shut off the electricity, and the cameras were set to night vision.

There were four men walking around on the first floor, searching from door to door with assault rifles raised and ready to fire.

The three who'd been unlucky enough to venture upstairs were lying dead on the stairs.

Enrique moved in a crouch, his adrenaline pumping at full speed. He went to the top of the stairs where one dead man lay with a nickel-sized hole in his forehead.

On the computer tablet, two more men had just met up at the foot of the staircase. Enrique guessed they were making plans to make it up the stairs without being gunned down like their three comrades.

Suddenly, the duo aimed their guns high.

Enrique stepped aside and put his back to the hallway wall just as bullets began flying his way.

The four masked gunmen on the first floor turned and sprinted toward the staircase.

Reaching around the wall and judging his aim off the iPad, Enrique started pulling the trigger.

BOOM. BOOM BOOM. BOOM BOOM BOOM BOOM BOOM BOOM.

Just like that, he ended the stairway standoff.

Both gunmen were slammed into the wall by the bullets that struck them.

Their four amigos made it to their dead bodies mere seconds later, and again bullets were sent soaring up toward Enrique as they came running up the stairs.

He had no idea how many rounds he had left but he knew that he must empty them all now if he wished to survive this attack, so again he reached around the wall and opened fire.

BOOM BOOM BOOM BOOM BOOM BOOM BOOM BOOM BOOM BOOM BOOM BOOM BOOM BOOM BOOM BOOM BOOM BOOM.

Then came the steady click of an emptied magazine. All thirty rounds had been depleted.

Three of the four were taken down, but the fourth man was still shooting and running up the stairs.

Drywall and chips of paint were exploding against the side of Enrique's face.

The man knew where he was standing, and he was all out of ammo. All of a sudden the gunshots ceased.

Enrique heard a dark laughter burst from the gunman. "No more bullets, eh?" the gunman shouted in Spanish. Enrique said nothing.

"I'll make this easy on you. Tell me where the lady and the little ones are and I'll let you live. Deal or no deal?"

Enrique remained silent, watching the iPad as the gunman made a slow approach.

"These are great friends of mine you took out, you son of a bitch. It's only right that I make you join them!"

Enrique underestimated the swiftness of the gunman; he thought he'd be able to reach out and grab ahold of the assault rifle with one hand and break the man's face with the other, but instead the masked man sidestepped as he made it to the top stair, and Enrique found himself staring down the barrel of the gun.

Chapter 32

Blake had intended to drive straight to Rita's place after dropping Remo off at the hospital.

Unfortunately, when the bullet-riddled tour bus made it to the Emergency Room at Cedars-Sinai Hospital, the LAPD was already ten cars deep in the parking lot.

They questioned everyone and searched the tour bus, but luckily all the weapons and drugs were already tucked away in Blake's duffle bag and in the many secret stash compartments throughout the coach.

Kendall talked to the policemen and told them what had gone down at the mansion. Nona and Bubbles gave statements.

Blake and the guys all refused to cooperate, claiming they were in shock and couldn't remember a single thing. The cops asked them about the Sunset Boulevard shooting and got the same response.

Police were dispatched to the mansion.

Twenty minutes later Sergio pulled up in a sparkling white Hummer limousine like nothing had happened to the Maybach he'd been driving a short while ago. Two black Audis full of new cartel soldiers were behind the Hummer.

With the tour bus now considered evidence in what would soon be named the city's most deadliest shooting in a decade, everyone but Remo (who was in the ER) got in the stretch Hummer, where Pedro was seated in back with

the two women he'd brought to the concert, and Sergio headed for Rita's place.

As soon as the flashing police lights were out of sight, the limousine's hardwood floor lifted and folded aside, and up rose a short table that was covered with gold-plated assault rifles, sparkling gold 50-round clips; golden .50-caliber Desert Eagle handguns that were encrusted with multicolored diamonds; an open kilo of cocaine bearing the Costilla Cartel's double C stamp; and piles upon piles of ten-thousand-dollar packets of bank-new Benjamin Franklins.

"I've got bad news," Pedro said somberly, staring at Blake with green, emotionless eyes. "We think they may have already reached Rita. I've been trying to call Enrique and the others who were there. No answer."

It felt like a sledgehammer struck Blake in the chest at that very moment; suddenly he could not breathe so well. His eyes began to water. His powerful black hands became clenched fists of fury. The only way he could think of releasing some frustration was to punch something.

So that is what he did.

He punched the window to the left of him, and all the glass shattered and blew out into the wind.

"Blake!" Bubbles and Nona exclaimed in complete unison.

He was gritting his teeth. Blood gushed forth from a deep cut in the side of his hand.

"Calm down, bruh," Meach said. He had brought his own cash-filled Louis Vuitton duffle bag, out of which he'd taken an ounce of Kush and a pack of cigarillos. He and Will Scrill were already rolling up blunts.

The Black girl who'd been Pedro's date at the concert said. "LA-fucking- X!" She and the Hispanic girl were dressed in expensive gowns and jewels, like Beverly Hills housewives.

Blake's pain-laden eyes landed on the girl and shut her up.

Pedro made himself a line of coke and rolled up a hundred-dollar bill. He sniffed it up a nostril and fell back in his seat.

Bubbles and Nona both had dark red eyes from the frightened tears they'd shed since the mansion shooting.

Nona was second to snort a line, but she waited until she had taken a scarf out of her purse and tied it around the gash in Blake's hand.

Though Blake hadn't done it in years, he became the third cocaine victim, and no one gave him shit about it because they understood his pain. He was

a father who no longer knew whether or not his children were alive and well. He was a stand-in boss for the wealthiest, most deadly drug cartel in history. He was a billionaire rap star who seemed to be a magnet for danger.

He made himself a second line of coke and sucked it up his other nostril.

He dialed Rita's phone number, got no answer, and decided to go for another line, but this time Nona stopped him.

"Slow down a little. You don't wanna be off your square at a time like this," she said.

Pedro's Hispanic female friend indulged in a line of the white stuff. Then Meach said fuck it and did two lines as well.

"We're going to kill every last one of those fucking traitors!" Pedro announced loud enough for passerby to hear. "No one gives a shit about the Zetas, or the Sinaloas, or the fucking dirty Gulf Cartel! None of those fuckers matter anymore! It's all about us! Me!" He jammed a thumb in his chest. "You!" He pointed at Blake. "Alexus! That's it! That's all that fucking matters anymore! We're the kings of the fucking world! Don't you worry about Rita and the little ones, my friend. If they have even a scratch on them, we'll cut off the heads of every fucking Zeta in Mexico! No more games, Blake. No more fucking Mr. Nice Guy! From here on out I'm going to be as hard on those fuckers as Papi was. They'll learn to bow down or face immediate execution. No questions, no regrets."

Blake was in no mood for conversation. Neither was he in the mood for a cup of Lean or a hit of Kush. Instead, he kept quiet and gulped down two shots of cognac.

When they finally made it to Rita's mansion, Blake slipped a fresh 30- round clip in his Glock and exited the limo behind the Hispanic girl.

He would always remember the traces of cocaine on the tip of her nose as she turned to look at him. She didn't say anything at first, just studied his face with her hands on her hips.

"Bulletface," she said finally. "It's sad that we had to meet under these circumstances, but at least I get to meet you. I'm a big fan."

Then there was a sharp crack in the night, and the Hispanic girl's head exploded in Blake's face.

King Rio

Chapter 33

"Sniper! There's a sniper! Run!" Pedro shouted.

Everyone took off running toward the mansion's front door, which Blake noticed was wide open as he hurriedly sprinted to it.

He felt something whizz past his right ear. A bullet.

He ducked his head and continued on as more whizzing bullets sailed by. "God, please let my kids be okay," he said aloud to himself as he hopped
over what he at first thought was some kind of lawn ornament.

Upon closer examination he saw that it was a dead man in a black suit.

One of the bodyguards assigned to protecting Rita and the kids. "Shit," he said as yet another bullet whizzed by.

The girl who'd angrily demanded they head to "LA-fucking-X" was screaming her head off as Pedro yanked her along behind him.

Blake wiped the Hispanic girl's blood and brain matter from his face as he made it to the door and lunged inside. He landed on Meach's back.

Several large-caliber bullets struck the door a second later, leaving huge holes as big and round as tennis balls in their wake.

Pedro fell in the door a moment later, screaming into his smartphone for his men to locate the sniper.

Wasting no time, Blake ran up the stairs, tripping over the bodies of dead men in his haste.

When he made it to the second floor, he ran straight to Vari's bedroom and found it empty.

He checked King's room. It too was vacant.

Then he went to Rita's bedroom, moving quickly and praying for his children's safety.

The door was shut.

He pushed it open and breathed a sigh of relief. Rita and the kids were sitting on the bed.

Enrique was sitting on the floor with his back against the wall. He was shirtless, and there was a bleeding hole in his abdomen.

"Daddy!" King and Vari yelled as they jumped from the bed and ran into Blake's arms.

He hugged them like he hadn't seen them in ages.

"She shot me," Enrique said, canting his head toward Rita.

"I saved him," Rita countered. "He ran out of bullets. I heard the guy mocking him for it. When I opened the door, the guy had a gun to Enrique's
head, about to kill him. I shot him a bunch of times, and Enrique happened to catch a bullet."

Blake didn't give a damn about Enrique's gunshot wound. He was just glad that his kids were safe.

Chapter 34

"Girl, check this out! It's going down with Bulletface in LA."

On Sasha's Facebook page, a friend had shared a news link that described a shooting on Sunset Boulevard involving Bulletface's tour bus, another mass shooting at the rapper's Los Angeles home that had left seventeen dead, and a third shooting at a mansion owned by Alexus Costilla that had resulted in eleven more murders.

Sasha was in the driver's seat of the Range Rover; Porsche had gotten tired of driving when they made it to the west side. They were parked behind a black S600 Benz in the dark alleyway on 15th Street, between Trumbull and Homan Avenues.

She handed Porsche the smartphone as Porsche passed her the blunt they were smoking. The transformation of Porsche's expression told Sasha that her friend was just as shocked by the news.

"That's that cartel shit," Porsche said. "I told you, those indictments Alexus is facing are real. I was around them for a long time. Those Mexican mothafuckas are way worse than the gangbangers we gotta deal with here in Chicago. They'll cut off your damn head and kill everybody in the house with you."

Shaking her head, Sasha glanced at her sideview mirror. Five boys were playing basketball in the alley, using a milk crate that was mailed to a wooden light pole next to someone's garage as a rim.

A second group of boys, gathered alongside the garage, were dealing drugs to the addicts who'd been coming and going since Sasha pulled up two hours prior.

They were waiting on the man who was going to buy two of the kilos of heroin from them for $60,000 apiece. His name was Cup, or Red D — apparently he was known by both. He'd promised to be here by midnight; that was two long hours ago.

"Glo is going to kill us if he finds us," Sasha said, taking her smartphone back. "I don't know if we should've took all his shit like that."

"Fuck him. Look at my forehead." Porsche had her seat reclined, blowing smoke out the sunroof. "I was a boss bitch before I met that nigga. I'm the reason he had all this dope and cash in the

149

first place. It's as much my money as it is his."

"Yeah, but still..."

"There's no fucking 'still'. I'm keeping it. Now, if you wanna give me your half back, by all means, feel free. I'll keep that, too. And the $120,000 we're getting from Cup. I'll keep it all, and you can take your ass back to Englewood."

Sasha sucked her teeth and rolled her eyes. She had a .40-caliber Ruger pistol on her lap, and she couldn't seem to stop looking in every direction.

"I don't trust these out west niggas, P. I'm comfortable out south." "Where niggas will kill you for nothin'?"

"Yeah, well, I ain't never been hurt." "Luckily."

Sasha coughed and leaned forward to put the blunt roach out.

"We're good over here," Porsche said. "We just hit a quarter-million-dollar lick. Niggas out south ain't seeing this kind of money. Not without going to the feds. Let's get this money, boo. Get us a house somewhere else and live life to the fullest."

Sasha nodded. "I just hope we never have to see that nigga Glo again. His ass is crazy, girl. You see what he did to you. I don't want my damn head busted, or worse..."

The threat of violence from Glo wasn't bothering Porsche. She wasn't even from out south anyway. The west side is where she'd been born and raised. She knew all the streets, all the alleys and gangways, all the dope boys, mob figures, hairstylists, bootleggers, boosters, and every other kind of man and woman on the west side streets.

A couple of minutes later, as Sasha was rolling what would be their fifth blunt, a pair of headlights illuminated the rearview mirror.

"That has to be him," Sasha said. "It's a white Lamborghini."

Porsche sat up to observe the car for herself. "Yeah, that's him. Listen, let me do all the talking. I know Cup personally. My sister used to fuck around with his best friend."

"What kinda talking? He should just be giving us the money and that's it.

Fuck a conversation. We got two kilos of heroin in here. Ain't no time to talk."

It was Porsche's turn to roll her eyes. "Just be quiet and let me do this, okay?"

Sasha issued another suck of the teeth but remained quiet as the Lamborghini crept up alongside them.

The Lamborghini's driver door lifted up in the air, and out stepped a tall, baldheaded light-skinned man in a white True Religion shirt and matching shorts. His Louboutin sneakers were white with gold spikes all over them. He had on a thick gold chain and a gold watch.

"Bitch, is he single," Sasha whispered as he reached in to a woman in his passenger seat and picked up an MCM duffle bag off her lap.

"Shut the fuck up." Porsche pushed open her door. She got out and gave Cup a hug, then returned to her seat as he opened the door behind her and climbed in.

"Who is that?" he asked immediately, looking at Sasha. "Nobody." Porsche smirked.

Again Sasha sucked her teeth.

"Pull out this hot ass alley." Cup handed the duffle to Porsche. "My sis gon' follow us in the Lambo. Drive down to Elbow's. The restaurant on 16th. I need to grab somethin' to eat. And where my shit?"

Porsche had the two kilos in a plastic bag between her feet; the rest of the dope, Kush, and cash was at the hotel room she and Sasha had gotten downtown before coming here to meet Cup. She took a look inside the duffle bag, saw that it was full of cash, and handed Cup the plastic bag with the kilos as Sasha drove off.

She started counting through the cash.

"Think I'm gon' short you or somethin'?" Cup asked with a laugh. "Not really. Just counting it."

"Where y'all get this shit from?"

"That's for me to know and you to find out," Porsche retorted. Sasha smiled at the witty reply.

"What's up wit' bruh-in-law?" Cup asked. He was talking about Blake. "You see all that shit goin' down in Cali?"

Porsche shrugged her shoulders dismissively. "Fuck that nigga. I got shot over his ass. I don't fuck with him or Alexus no more."

"Yeah, some Puerto Rican niggas tried to wack him at my club last night.

I had to shut down because of that shit." "They should've

killed his punk ass."

"Nah, don't say that. Blake's a good nigga. I wouldn't be rich now if it wasn't for him and Alexus. I'm hoping she comes out of that coma."

"That makes one of us. As far as I'm concerned the bitch can die." Cup laughed. "You shouldn't have drugged that man."

"Fuck him"

"You're somethin' else."

"Whatever. They should've given me and my sister way more money than the little bit of change they gave us. It's their fault my momma's dead, and it's their fault my sister's kids got killed. Fucking around with them we lost everybody. Even my sister's baby daddy got killed. I hate Alexus. Her and her punk ass husband can go to hell."

"You don't mean that." "The hell I don't."

Cup laughed shook Porsche's headrest. "You're a certified lunatic, you know that?"

"It's a cold world." She told Sasha to make a right onto 16th Street. "I might be leaving Chicago for good in the morning...depending on what my girl wants to do. Even if she doesn't wanna go, I'm leaving. I'm sick of this crazy drama all the goddamn time. Let me move to Miami for a year or two. Fuck it. Or New York. I hear it's fun out there."

Cup sniffed the air. "Where is that weed at? Smell like that loud pack." "I only brought a few blunts with me. We got some for sale, though.

Actually, we got a couple pounds."

"Damn, y'all done came up out here, huh? Y'all stick a nigga up or somethin'? For real. How you get this shit?"

Sasha was pulling up in front of the restaurant. It was one of the few spots that stayed open 24/7 in the Lawndale neighborhood.

There were gang members — Porsche guessed they were Vice Lords, either Travelers or Conservatives — standing with three girls around two raggedy old cars out front.

A Chicago police car cruised smoothly through the intersection's red light and frightened Porsche, but soon it was out of sight.

She noticed that the Lamborghini was was pulling up behind her Range Rover, and suddenly she found herself wondering who the girl was, whether

our not the girl was really Cup's "sis" or just another thot infatuated with Cup's wealth.

Cup seemed to read her mind. "That's like my sister. It's really Lil Cholly's sister, but you know that's my lil bruh. She just opened a bowling alley out in Lincoln Park. I own half of it, but it's hers."

"It's not hers if you own half of it," Porsche said matter-of-factly. "She'll pay me off and then it'll be hers. Same thing."

"No the hell it's not." Porsche turned in her seat and gazed at Cup. He was typing a message on his smartphone.

"Telling sis what to get me," he said. "Y'all want something?"

"We just ate at McDonald's again, waiting on your good time-telling ass for two hours," Sasha said.

Cup sent the text and put the phone in his pocket. He laughed at Sasha's comment but gave her no response.

Porsche kept gazing at Cup. "Why are you hoping Alexus is okay?" she inquired, studying his features for a reaction. "Didn't that bitch shoot you the day her momma was nailed to a cross by that terrorist bitch Jenny Costilla? And I heard about you kidnapping Blake's daughter a while back. Heard him and Alexus talking about it. So why are you all of a sudden so friendly with them?"

"Business is business," was Cup's succinct explanation.

Porsche had an idea. "What if I told you they have plans for you? What would you say to that?"

"Depends on what kinda plans you're talking." "Plans to get you back for kidnapping Savaria." He shrugged and waited for her to explain.

"Blake is sending somebody at you soon. That's all I know. So be safe." Porsche turned away from him and started stuffing the rubber-banded bundles of cash from the duffle into her own Gucci shoulder bag and handing Sasha the cash that wouldn't fit; she and Sasha were matching today.

"Who told you that?" Cup asked.

"Who do you think told me?" She reached around her seat with his empty duffle bag and gave it to him. "I'll catch up with you later. Call me. I'll be around."

"Hold up." Cup's voice became authoritative. He dropped the bricks of heroin in the duffle bag and zipped it shut. "Tell me who told you that."

Porsche fought back the urge to smile as she studied her fingernails. Sasha was staring at her, knowing exactly what she was up to.

"I'm serious, Porsche. That's not something I can just let go. You gotta tell me who said that shit. Put me up on game so I don't fuck around and slip up, you feel me?"

She gave an understanding nod. "Yeah, I feel you." "Well...? Who said it?"

She sighed. "Look, you can't tell them I told you, but Blake is supposed to be paying some nigga named Glo to shoot you. I don't think Glo's going to do it but it'll probably be one of his guys, the BD's from Parkway Gardens. Chief Keef's squad, you know who I'm talking about."

"I know Glo." Cup spoke in a near whisper, thoughtfully pinching the piece of skin under his bottom lip. "You heard em say that shit?"

"Mmm hmm. I think it's about time for Blake's ass to go out like Pac and Biggie. He's doing too much."

"When did you hear him say it?"

"Last week sometime, can't remember which day. I was out there in Los Angeles to visit my sister in the hospital. He was there for Alexus. Heard him on the phone with Glo. You really need to get both of them taken care of. That's what I'd do. There's no room for mistakes when you've got two real goons tryna take you out the game."

Cup bit down on his lower lip and thought a moment longer. Then he opened his door and stepped out.

"I'll be calling later," he said, and headed for the Lambo, lighting a cigarette and strolling as if the two kilos of heroin were merely bricks of flour.

"You are something else," Sasha said, pulling off.

"I'm a smart bitch, that's all," Porsche said. "You'll thank me for all this shit later."

Chapter 35

The following weekend, Blake, Rita, and the kids sat on the front deck of The Omnipotent, the now 700-foot megayacht worth hundreds of millions of dollars that Juan "Papi" Costilla had purchased years earlier and left to Alexus upon his unfortunate death.

They were drifting in the Pacific Ocean off the coast of Malibu, California, Rita reading her Bible on an iPad, King Neal, and Savaria chatting back and forth about a Superman movie, Blake kicked back in a lounge chair with his diamond-encrusted headphones on, listening to the summer jam that had become his favorite over the past few months — Chedda Da Connect's "Flicka Da Wrist".

Blake wore a pair of yellow Nike gym shorts and matching Air Max sneakers. His headphones were plugged into his iPad, which minutes ago he'd been using to shop for a set of new Forgiato rims for the Bentley convertible he'd bought a few days prior. Today he didn't have on any jewelry, aside from the gold and diamonds on his teeth. His hands were interlaced behind his head. His eyes—cloaked beneath Louis Vuitton sunglasses — were gazing out over the vast ocean waters.

King ran over and leapt onto Blake, dropping his knees onto his father's chiseled abdomen.

Blake groaned in displeasure. "You lil..."

King laughed. "You almost said a bad word, Daddy." "You almost got your ass whooped."

"Oooooh!" King put his hand over his mouth. "Momma gon hurt you when her get out from the hopsital."

"It's called a hospital, not a hopsital." "That's what I said. The hopsital."

Blake laughed and shook his son by the shoulders. "King Neal...what am I going to do with you?"

"Buy me a new bike." Blake cracked up laughing.

"I'm for real, Daddy. Vari always get bikes for her birthdays."

"You'll be fine without another bike, King. You have, what, seven of em now?"

"This many." King held up four fingers.

"You's a 'this many' lie. I bought you four bikes last year

155

alone." "But I want the new one."

"You gon' get a new ass whoopin' if you don't go on somewhere," Blake jokingly threatened.

Savaria popped up beside Blake. "Daddy, why you never whoop him?

He's always bad. You should whoop him every day."

"Maybe," Blake suggested, "I should whoop you every day too. Think that would help you to stop being a brat?"

"Hey, I'm not a brat!" Vari refuted. Blake gaped his eyes in disagreement.

Vari lifted the side of her lip in disgust. "I can't wait for Ma to get out the hospital. She'll take up for me the way you do with King." She sucked her teeth.

Blake laughed and swooped his son into his arms. "It's us against the girls, King. You with me?"

King nodded, all smiles, and Vari planted her hands on her hips the way Alexus and Rita always did and pouted.

"I hate y'all," she said.

Blake grinned. "Why? We love you." "Y'all don't love me."

"Yes, we do. Don't we, King? Don't we love your Ma and your sister?"

King was all smiles. "Nope!" He crossed his arms over his small chest and laughed heartily.

Vari gave him a hard slap on the leg and ran off to Rita's side.

Suddenly frowning, King turned to his father, rubbing his leg. "Her hit me," he said.

"She hit you, not her." "She hit me."

"You snitchin', lil nigga? What I tell you 'bout that snitchin'? Huh?"

King Neal got quiet then, for he knew that snitching was against the rules and would undoubtedly get him in more trouble than he'd ever been in.

"Let me tell you a story," Blake said, sitting up in his seat. "You have to promise to always remember it, okay? Forever. You promise?"

King nodded once.

"Once upon a time," Blake began, "there was a snitch and a real boy. Now, the real boy saw that the snitch had gotten into a fight with some other boys. The snitch told the teacher that all the boys punched him, and he said the real boy had witnessed all of it. What did the real boy say when the teacher asked him what was going on?"

King seemed to think for a long moment; then: "I don't know, Daddy." "You're right. The real boy didn't know what happened. Even though he had seen it all happen, he didn't tell anybody. And do you know why?"

"Because he was a real boy and because real boys don't tell," King said, remembering the countless times he'd listened to the exact same lesson.

Blake kept him on a tight leash. He didn't want his boy mingling with the wrong crowds, taking on the wrong traits. Being a tattletale was dangerous for a man. Especially a black man. Blake knew men who'd been killed for saying too much.

Blake high-fived his son (King loved high-fives, they always made him laugh for some reason) just as five women and a boy that was King's age came walking onto the deck.

The women were wearing bathing suits and drinking from salt-rimmed cocktail glasses full of tequila. They were Baddie Barbie, Bubbles, Nona, Tiff-Tiff, and Danielle.

A week ago, the little boy's name had been Timothy; since learning of the child's paternity, Blake had had Timothy's name changed to Blake King, Jr.

Junior looked almost identical to King Neal. Blake took delight in the similarities.

"Go play with your brother and sister," Blake said as he gave King Neal a slap to the back of the head and sent him on his way.

Blake settled his eyes on Barbie as she and the other women sauntered toward him, and suddenly he was glad that he'd chosen to wear sunglasses; his questioning squint would go unnoticed.

He didn't know how to feel about Barbie's betrayal in Hollywood. She claimed to have done nothing with Breezy but Blake didn't believe her. It wasn't that he was hurt over her fucking another guy. It was that he didn't trust her. Especially knowing that he'd shot and killed her sister and that she had only come around him to find out what had really happened.

He shifted his eyes to Bubbles and Nona, gawked at their

amazing curves, and then looked at Tiff. His lawyer had already done all the legal papers involving child support. The court ruled he owed $10.8 million in backpay and $225,000-a-month. He'd paid the backpay immediately, and Tiff-Tiff had moved straight to Atlanta with her friend Danielle. She'd bought a nice- sized mansion there. There was a boyfriend, but Blake didn't care. As long as Junior was good, Blake was good.

"This is the biggest damn boat I've ever been on," Bubbles said with a glorious smile. "You got jet skis on this bitch, an inflatable slide, a helicopter on the roof, bedrooms, a kitchen, a gym, a theater. I can't name a room it doesn't have. I could live on here."

"It ain't mine," Blake reminded her. "It's my wife's." "Whoever's it is, this hoe is fly."

A drab chuckle escaped Blake's throat as he stood up and took off his headphones. Nona nearly bit through her bottom lip as she lusted over his sharply defined abs. He could almost see the extra saliva form in Tiff-Tiff's mouth.

He grinned. "Y'all some thirsty lil thotties," he said.

"Don't call me no thot," Nona snapped playfully. "Come on, take us on those jet skis. I've never rode one before."

"I got a jet ski you can ride." Blake's grin was unending.

"Asshole," Tiff laughed. "We're for real, now, come on, boy. Meach n'em acting like they don't even wanna leave the gym."

Meach, Biggs, Young, and Will Scrill were getting a workout in in the indoor gymnasium. Blake had awakened earlier than everyone else; his 45- minute workout had been done alone.

"I'm not getting on no jet skis right now," he said. "I'm thinking about my wife."

"Why," Bubbles asked, "because her mom is sitting over there?"

He shook his head no. "Her birthday's coming up, and she's still in that coma. They say it's a medicinal coma now, just for surgery and stuff, I guess. She should be back with us soon."

"You think she's going to the feds?" Tiff asked.

Blake shrugged. He didn't have a clue as to what would happen when Alexus Costilla came out of the coma. He hoped she'd be given a bond, like Pedro had been given. He hoped she'd be able to get back to business as soon as possible so that he could finally get away from all cartel drama. He hoped she wouldn't spend the rest of her life in prison. He hoped she'd still love him, the way he still loved her, even though they were no longer an item.

Hope.

It's all he had.

He gave in and took the girls and the kids riding on the jet skis. Soon they were joined by Meach and Biggs; Will Scrill and Young couldn't swim.

When he was giving Nona her fourth ride, she asked him if he was going to a party Cup had invited him to in Chicago this coming weekend.

He shrugged. It took him a moment to answer.

"I don't really trust that nigga too much. He had something to do with my daughter getting kidnapped. I think he might've killed my baby mama. If he didn't, he had it done. If I wasn't making so much money with the nigga I would've murked him a long ass time ago."

"Remember I used to work for him. At The Visionary Lounge. He was a grimy ass nigga but he's about his money. Gotta give it to him." She rested her chin on Blake's shoulder. "You think he's up to some more bullshit?"

"Ain't no telling. I'm really tryna stay away from any and all kinds of drama. That shit with the cartel got me feeling crazy about a lot of shit. I wanna live. I want my family to live. If I can I wanna get to heaven eventually, you feel me? I don't wanna die."

"You'll live, Blake. You're Bulletface. Nobody can fuck with you." "Just because I'm Bulletface doesn't mean I'm bulletproof."

"Yeah, but you got the money to bulletproof everything you wear and everything you drive if need be. You'll be fine. Fuck it, if you don't feel right about it, then don't go. It is odd that he would just out the blue invite you to a party. His ass ain't been inviting you nowhere."

"I know." Blake jumped a huge wave; and Nona squeezed him tight around the waist and screamed. "Stop yellin' in my mu-hfuckin ear before I throw yo' ass off this jet ski," he said jokingly.

"Boy, take me back to the yacht. That shit just scared the life outta me."

King Rio

Chapter 36

Baddie Barbie's smile was as fake as a three-dollar bill as she picked up her Birkin bag and excused herself to the bathroom.

Once away from everyone, she explored the vast floor of the yacht before settling in the theater and turning on the screen. She was surprised to find that the movie was actually a porn. Cherokee D'Ass and Pinky were smashing some white guy's head between their butts.

She dug in her purse for her iPhone and dialed her sister Fantasia's number. It rang until the voicemail came on. She hung up and called again and got the same result.

She was just about to leave a voicemail when Fantasia called back. "What's up, lil sis," Fantasia said, sounding like she didn't want to be
bothered.

Tasia "Baddie Barbie" Olsen knew why.

When Blake had thrown her into his bathroom mirror in Chicago, she hadn't told her sister. In fact, she'd lied, claiming that a group of girls had jumped her at the club. Fantasia knew when her little sister was lying. She'd seen right through the lie, but Tasia had stuck to it.

They hadn't talked ever since.

"Bitch, you saw me calling," Tasia said.

"Are you falling in love with that nigga Bulletface?" "Hell fucking no."

"Did you forget that our sister is missing and considered dead? And that she was lay seem with him and Alexus?"

"Will you please shut up and listen to me for a minute? Damn. Let me get a word in."

"No, bitch, you was supposed to be fucking with that nigga to find out if he knows what happened to Janny. That's it. You said you was gonna kill the bastard. Whatever happened to that? Seems to me like everybody in the world is trying to kill his ass, but nooooo, not you. You're all laid up with the nigga. Bitch, is the dick that good? Huh? Are you dick-whipped or some shit? Because it sure in the hell seems like it."

Barbie sighed and pinched the bridge of her nose in frustration.

Fantasia sailed on: "You told me you was gon' find out what

went down in Mexico and kill that nigga if he was involved. Tell me what you've heard so far. I wouldn't be surprised if the nigga done admitted the shit already."

Barbie took a deep breath and then spoke. "He...when he found out who I was, he...he's the one who busted my head. He threw me into a mirror."

"You stupid bitch." "I know, I —"

"So, he just threw you up against a mirror as soon as you told him your name? And you don't think the nigga did something to Janny?"

"I didn't tell him. He Googled it."

"Bitch, I don't give a fuck how he found out your goddamn name! It's about what he did when he found out! You mean to tell me you lied to me about who has you walking around with staples in your damn head, knowing that it was because of who you're related to!"

"I messed up. I know." Barbie sighed again. "I'll take care of that nigga, okay? No problem. No worries. Just give me some time."

"You're letting his money and fame get to your head. Fuck that nigga!

More than likely, he killed our sister! Are you retarded or something! Don't call my phone again unless it's to tell me that bitch ass nigga is dead. Bye!"

Fantasia hung up without giving Barbie a chance to say another word.

For a few seconds, Barbie stared emptily at the phone. Her sister was right and she knew it. Her relationship with Blake had clouded her judgment.

He'd been giving her so much money lately. And Fanny was right— the nigga's dick game did have her sprung. But it wasn't supposed to get this far. She'd planned to figure out if he was involved in her sister's disappearance and then put an end to him if he was.

Somewhere along the way she'd gone astray.

She was just about to stand up and head back out to the deck when Blake's voice startled her.

"You'll take care of that nigga? Who is 'that nigga'?" She

turned and saw him standing in the doorway.

Jesus Christ, she thought. How long had he been standing there listening? "Boy, you scared me," she said, because nothing else came to mind.

He walked to her and looked down at her phone. "Who was that?" "My sister."

"Who is the nigga you say you gon' take care of?"

"Some fuck nigga in Atlanta. An ex boyfriend of mine. He came over and stole my sister's rent money. She's hot as fish grease about it."

"Yeah?" Blake's eyes were disbelieving.

Barbie nodded her head yes, shocked by how quickly the lie had spilled from her lips.

She half-expected him to pick up her phone and redial the last number she'd called.

Instead, he looked at the movie screen and said, "You's a lil freak." "I didn't put that in! I just turned it on."

"Yeah right."

"I'm not lying. You need to review these cameras you got all around here.

It might've been your son's little mannish ass. That lil boy grabbed my booty yesterday."

Blake laughed. His eyes stayed on the movie screen a moment longer.

Taking the opportunity to shift his mind from the phone call, Barbie yanked down the front of his shorts and gave his long, limp penis a lick.

His attention instantly went back to her.

She didn't say a word, choosing instead to suck the head into her mouth and to stroke his length in her hands.

He grew hard in a matter of seconds. Soon he was holding her head and ramming his dick deep down her throat, gazing down at her pretty face with his bottom lip tucked in his mouth and his upper teeth glittering in the reflection of the ceiling lights.

"Fuck yo' ex boyfriend," he said. "That nigga ain't got shit on me." She kept sucking him.

"I wanna bust all in yo' mouth and watch you swallow that shit. You gon' do that for me? You gon' do that for a real nigga?"

She nodded her head yes. She had only swallowed cum once in

her life but she would do it again today. For Bulletface she would. After all, he deserved a good sucking before he went to his grave. He lasted all of five minutes.

Just as his thick semen began gushing out over her tongue, Alexus Costilla's mother appeared in the doorway, holding her wide hips and looking at Blake and Barbie like they were the scum of the earth.

Barbie saw it out of the corner of her eye, but Blake didn't seem to notice, and a second later the woman was gone.

She sucked and squeezed out the last drops of cum before dropping her head back and opening wide to show him the mouthful of protein he'd given her.

Then she swallowed with a tight face.

Blake never mentioned the phone call again, and when they made it back outside with everyone else, Rita and Blake's private helicopter pilot were soaring away in the chopper.

Chapter 37

The skies of El Paso cried at Lisa's burial.

Pedro watched from his window in the rear of his now-repaired Rolls- Royce Phantom Drophead Coupe as Sergio drove through Concordia Cemetery to Lisa's burial site.

He'd sent an anonymous donation of $50,000 to Lisa's parents to cover the funeral expenses. He also paid off the mortgage on their home in Kansas and bought the distraught couple a new Lexus SUV.

Serg parked behind a Ford minivan near the burial service, and from there Pedro watched in silence.

It didn't take him long to spot Mary.

She was standing near the parents, clad in a wide-brim hat over a short black dress and heels. She had her back to him, but he knew without a shadow of a doubt that it was indeed her.

The privacy partition rolled down. Sergio turned and looked back at Pedro.

"See her?" he asked. Pedro nodded.

"She's the hot piece of ass in that birthday dress over there, ain't she?" "Shut up, Serg."

"Hey, hey, hey...I'm just saying. She's a hot piece. No disrespect. All I'm saying is I'd date the black chick in a heartbeat. She's my kind of girl."

"How about you roll that window back up before I do you some serious harm."

Sergio laughed. He knew Pedro was only kidding. "You've really got the hots for this girl, don't you? What is it? I mean, what makes you want her the way you do? Can't be because she's black. I've seen you with a black girl before. Remember the famous actress you had that one time in Cancun? What was her name?"

"She wasn't an actress. You're talking about Jazmine. She was a film director."

"Same difference. She was pretty hot, wouldn't you say?"

Pedro held down the button that raised the partition. He watched Serg crack up laughing until the tinted glass closed.

It was twenty minutes later when Lisa's casket was finally lowered into the ground. By then the steady drizzle of rain had turned into a full downpour.

King Rio

When Mary came running toward a small Mercedes that was parked three car-lengths ahead of Pedro's Phantom, holding her hat on with one hand, he stepped out with his umbrella and beat her to the driver door.

"Allow me," he said, his fingers curling in the door handle. She looked at him and froze.

He pulled open the door for her. Her eyes never left his as she got in and slammed the door shut. He walked around to the passenger door, half-expecting her to lock it before he reached it, but she made no move to stop him as he got in next to her.

"Nice car," he said.

She only looked at him.

"Listen," he began, "I know, I should have just left you both in Mexico where I found you. It was never my intention for something like this to happen. You know that. There's no way either of us could have known that a fucking sniper would be at Rita's place when we got there. I couldn't have foreseen that, and you know it."

He looked to her for a response but none came. She just sat there, rain dripping down from the brim of her hat. He couldn't tell if the wet streaks on her face were tears or precipitation.

"Don't just stare at me, Mary. Tell me something."

"What do you want from me?" Her words were cold and very much to the point. "Why are you here?"

"To see you."

"Okay, well, nice seeing you."

His eyes stayed on her, waiting for more, but nothing came for half a minute.

Finally, she rested her forehead on the woodgrain steering wheel and let out a heavy sigh. Pedro noticed an empty baggie in the ashtray that had traces of white powder in it.

"I don't blame you for anything," Mary said, sobbing. "If anything you saved Lisa in Juarez. And it's not like you put a gun to our heads and forced us to ride with you. You paid us. Paid us good, too. I wouldn't have this car if it wasn't for you, or the house I'm moving into. I just bonded my brother out of jail with some of the money you gave me. You helped me a lot more than you hurt me."

166

She lifted her head. Pedro picked a tissue out of the Kleenex box on her dashboard and wiped her eyes with it.

"I've never had someone help me for nothing, you know that? Everybody wanted something from me in return. And then I met you, and in twenty- four hours you gave me more than any man has ever given me. And I was such a snob that I didn't even say thanks."

"You didn't need to, Mary. I did it all out of the kindness of my heart. You don't owe me anything. Not a thank you, not an apology— nothing." He

placed a hand on the middle of her back and gave it a rub. "Come on. Drive. Everyone's leaving. Serg will follow us."

It took her a minute to straighten her face but eventually she got it together and started the car. She drove off ahead of the Rolls-Royce, dabbing at her eyes with the tissue.

"Can I see the place?" Pedro asked.

She shrugged her shoulders. "Sure. I don't care. It's just a three bedroom.

Nothing like those castles you're used to." They both laughed at the same time.

"That's it," Pedro said, rubbing her back again. "Cheer up. Laugh a little. Smile for your friend. I'm sure she wouldn't want you crying like a baby."

"I'll be fine."

"I know that. I won't let you be anything but fine. Even if you don't want me around, from here on out I'm going to make sure you're okay every single day of your life."

King Rio

Chapter 38

In the days following, Blake spent a lot of time between Atlanta and Chicago, both in the studio and at Tiff's house. Junior got used to having a brother his age and a big sister almost overnight. Everyone in the Atlanta area wanted to know who Tiffany Jenkins was and how she'd ended up having a baby by their favorite rapper.

One night, while popping bottles in VIP at Club Crucial, his fellow rapper and friend T.I.'s nightclub, Blake met a woman named Fanny who looked a lot like Barbie.

Barbie just so happened to be in the club with him that night.

"You might as well take me home with you so I can show you what this nookie do," Fanny said.

"Yeah?" Blake looked at Barbie. "You with it?" "I'm down," Barbie said.

"Fuck it, it's a date." Blake laughed and rubbed his hands together like Birdman in anticipation of what was to come.

He was getting ready to fly to Chicago for the party Cup had invited him to. He'd heard that Lil Durk, Lanipop, and some new rapper named Glo was going to be there.

He would take Barbie and the new girl with him. It would be fun.

Or at least that's what he thought it would be.

To Be Continued...
The Cocaine Princess 9
Coming Soon

Keep reading for a sneak peak of The Cocaine Princess 9!

King Rio

Prologue

It was 10:17 on the morning of her 23rd birthday, April 21st, 2015, when Alexus Costilla came out of the coma.

Rita Mae Bishop, her mother, was sitting in an easy chair next to her bed, so busy reading the Bible that she didn't realize Alexus's eyes had opened.

There was a powerfully-built white man standing under the wall-mounted television across from her bed. He wore slacks and a navy blue blazer with FBI stenciled over the left breast in big yellow letters.

Two more FBI agents were standing at the big wooden door at the entrance of her hospital room.

She tried to remember how she'd gotten here and couldn't think of a thing.

Her last memory was an argument with her husband, Blake "Bulletface" King, a rapper whose name was synonymous with Jay Z and Lil Wayne. He had put his gun to her sister Mercedes's head with the intent to shoot her dead for allegedly setting him up, and Alexus had pulled her own gun on him to save her sister.

She remembered seeing Blake leave, but nothing else came to mind. "Alexus!" Rita shouted excitedly when she saw that Alexus was awake. Alexus tried to voice a reply but all that came out was a hoarse whisper:

"Where... Blake..."

"Sshhh." Rita walked to the bedside, lifted Alexus's hand in hers, and pressed her lips to her daughter's forehead. "You've got a tube down your throat. Relax. Blake just left with Meach and Biggs. He's got a show in Chicago he has to make it to. Enrique is out in the waiting area with Pedro."

Alexus felt weak. Weak and heavily sedated. She looked at her left arm and saw stitches in several different places. Her left leg and foot were bandaged. She moved her right arm and heard a metallic clink.

Her wrist was handcuffed to the bedrail.

"Sit still, baby," Rita said. "Just sit still. The Lord has you wrapped in his arms."

"Blake..."

"Hold on, I'll call him." Rita dialed a number on her

smartphone and put it on speakerphone.

"What's up, Momma." Blake's voice calmed Alexus instantly.

"Alexus just woke up. Talk. She can hear you."

Blake paused; then, "I love you, baby." Alexus smiled.

"I'm on my way back to the airport now," he continued. "I was about to get on the jet and fly to Chicago. I got a concert out there tonight. Be strong, okay? They'll probably be taking you to jail but don't worry, we'll get you right out. The judge gave you a forty-million-dollar bond. They indicted almost everybody right after the suicide bombing. Britney will get the bond paid and you'll be home asap."

Alexus managed to utter one final word: "Mexico." Both Rita and Blake understood what she meant.

Alexus Costilla was the boss of the Costilla Cartel, a Mexican drug cartel that now included every major cartel in Mexico.

She wanted to go to Mexico, where her family had ruled for years, and where she was now considered the ultimate queen of the drug trade.

Chapter 1

Three hours and forty million dollars later Alexus Costilla left the Los Angeles courthouse in a wheelchair that was made of 24-karat gold and encrusted with white diamonds. Knowing her taste for the finer things in life, Enrique had paid top dollar for the customized wheelchair weeks earlier, shortly after the suicide bombing that had hospitalized her and her sister and cost Enrique his left hand.

Alexus's sparkling fleet of seven snow white Rolls-Royce Phantoms were parked at the curb. News correspondents from every major television network were waiting out front with cameras and microphones, and they immediately began shouting questions.

"Alexus, what do you have to say about the charges being brought against you?"

"Are you really a cartel boss, as the indictments allege?"

"Is it true that you and Bulletface have called it quits?"

"If you two get divorced, will you share custody of both children?" "Have you heard about the new kid?"

"How has the news of your uncle Flako's death affected you?"

Alexus had no comment. Her attorney, Britney Bostic, waved the reporters off.

As soon as Alexus and her mother were situated in the backseat of one of the Phantoms, her driver headed straight for the airport.

The now-removed feeding tubes that had been her source of food for the past month and a half had Alexus's throat sore. She sipped half mouthfuls of water at a time and winced with every swallow. Her stitches itched. The burns on her leg itched.

"Everything's fine," Rita kept saying.

Alexus just stared out her window and sipped more water. She was in pain. Her left wrist had been lacerated and broken in the explosion. She had a hundred and forty-seven stitches and fifty-three staples in her body, and third-degree burns on her left leg.

It would be a long recovery, she knew. One that would be painful and difficult but certainly possible.

"Blake's in charge of everything now," Enrique said from the passenger seat as he lowered his window a crack and put fire to the end of a Cuban cigar. "He's handling it all pretty well. Made you another $180 million already. He's like that Big Meach guy we

173

used to deal with, only ten times wealthier. Our product has taken over most of the country. He's even nudging his way into Colorado's legal marijuana market with four shops opening there in the coming months. Some guy named Glo shot at him about a week ago in Chicago, and he went through hell dealing with Gamuza in LA, but he's doing great. He just sent me a text saying he's waiting to see you at the airport."

"Forget Blake," Alexus said. "He keeps fucking cheating on me."

Rita nodded her head. She had her trusty old Bible peeking out of the black leather Birkin bag on the lap of her black Prada sundress. Fifty carats of refulgent white diamonds were shining in the custom designed Chanel tennis bracelet on her left wrist. She too had burns, old burns on the left side of her face from when Alexus's aunt Jenny Costilla had detonated a bomb on her front porch, but the scarred tissue was unnoticeable beneath her makeup. Her hair was done in a short, neat bob. Her piercing brown eyes worriedly studied Alexus, while Alexus continued to gaze thoughtfully out her window, seemingly unfazed by all that was going on.

"Aren't you upset?" Rita asked. "Hurt? Anything. You look like you're at peace when clearly peace is not what we're experiencing. And now Blake's been sleeping with some ratchet stripper girl from Atlanta. Her name's Barbie. You cannot be at ease. I'm here, baby. I know you're grown and all but you'll always be my baby. Talk to me."

Alexus took a brief moment to reply; the news of Blake cheating again momentarily stopped her breath. "Just get me to Mexico," she said finally, fighting back a flood of tears. "I'm done with him, anyway. He pulled a gun on my sister. I'll let him keep running the cartel. Let him give all the orders and deal with the savages. I'll get money off his black ass until one of the other bosses gets tired of him. They'll take care of him one day but we're done. I'm getting a divorce. "

"That's King and Vari's father, Alexus. He's the father of your kids. You know Vari will not live without her brother."

Alexus took another swig of water and gave Rita an incredulous look. A teardrop cascaded down from her left eye and paused for two seconds on the middle of her cheek before continuing down to her chin. "You divorced Papi."

"Not for cheating."

"A lie is a lie," Alexus countered.

For this Rita had no reply. She had divorced Alexus's father — deceased Costilla Cartel boss Juan "Papi" Costilla — when he had come clean about his involvement with the Costilla Cartel, and once he was indicted on federal drug charges and arrested in a raid on their home, she'd taken Alexus and left him for good.

It was ironic that Alexus was now the boss of the Costilla Cartel. "Your sister left the hospital last week ago," Rita said. "She's back in

Chicago and staying with Porsche for now."

Blake's black Maybach was parked in between two white Mercedes vans in the hangar when they made it to LAX and pulled up beside one of the Boeing 767s that Alexus used to transport her vehicles around the world with her while she relaxed in her Gulfstream 650 private jet, usually spending money online in one way or another.

Leaning back on the hood of the gaudy foreign car, Blake wore a black Balmain shirt over matching jeans. Louis Vuitton's "LV" logos decorated

his sneakers, belt, and skullcap. Three letters — MBM, which stood for Money Bagz Management, his record label — made up the black diamond- encrusted pendants that hung from his two long gold and white diamond necklaces. There were round-cut white diamonds gleaming in his Hublot watch and bracelet. Larger white diamonds shined on his two pinkie rings. Even his teeth — recently changed from platinum to gold — were blinging with white diamonds. He held a double cup of Lean in his right hand, a fat blunt in the other.

Three MBM rap artists — Will Scrill, Young Meach, and Biggs, all dressed just as gaudily and each holding their own cups and blunts — were standing around Blake.

All of them looked at the fleet of Rolls-Royces until the Phantoms parked.

Sergio, Enrique's round-bodied nephew, pulled the wheelchair out of the trunk and rolled it around to Alexus's door. Blake set his cups down on the shiny hood of his Maybach and rushed over to help her into the wheelchair.

"Happy Birthday, baby," he said, pecking his lips on the middle of her forehead as she settled in and gazed at him with frigid eyes.

A wheelchair accessible ramp was resting against the Gulfstream's open door, and standing alongside it were twelve armed men in black suits and sunglasses.

Alexus scowled at Blake. "I fucking hate you, do you know that? And who's the stripper? What's her fucking name?"

Blake grinned and took a step back. "Nobody."

"I don't care who she is. I'm not gonna get her killed. You enjoy yourself.

You and that bitch. I'll file for divorce later this week. We can share custody."

She saw the harsh reality of their break-up register on Blake's face. He loved both of his children; losing either of them in a custody battle would emotionally wound him, and Alexus knew it.

He paused for a long moment. By the time he spoke, Rita was out of the Rolls and standing behind the wheelchair.

"We'll talk later," he said finally.

"You'll talk to my lawyers," Alexus countered. "You can run the family business for now, but only until I'm healthy enough to manage things myself. Then I don't ever wanna see you again unless you're picking up the kids. Comprende?"

Blake said nothing.

Stone-faced, he stared after Alexus as Sergio wheeled her to the private jet and up the ramp. She glanced back several times but had no regrets.

Her main focus was getting physically fit again and going back to being the boss of the drug world.

She didn't need Blake to do that.

Chapter 2

More than two hundred armed soldiers and high-ranking Costilla Cartel members were standing alongside the private landing strip behind Alexus's megamansion in Matamoros, Mexico when her Gulfstream jet landed.

Alexus paid them no mind. Rita helped her into a waiting Range Rover and two minutes later they were in her ten-car garage.

Wheeling Alexus into the mansion, Rita said, "Don't let what's going on with Blake stress you out. You don't need stress at a time like this. You need to be healing. Let Jesus heal your wounds and your heart. You'll be fine."

Alexus was swallowing more water when her son, King Neal Costilla, came running to her, followed by his nine-year-old big sister Savaria King, Blake's daughter from a previous relationship, and Tamera, their babysitter.

"Mommyyyyyy!" King Neal screamed, smiling from ear to ear. He hugged Alexus gently. "I love you, Ma!"

"I love you, too, Ma," Savaria added. She always called Alexus her mother. Her biological mother had been killed years prior.

Rita pushed the wheelchair to the high-ceilinged family room. The kids walked alongside Alexus, already talking her ear off. King spoke of a fight he'd had with Vari yesterday; Vari claimed it wasn't a fight and it definitely wasn't yesterday. Vari said she and King had been having a lot of fun riding their horses lately; King said yeah, he'd had fun... until he'd fallen off the back of his horse and hurt his arm.

"It was her fault!" he said, pointing an accusatory finger at Tamera, who snickered and replied,

"Hey, I told you to hold on."

A 24-karat gold Monopoly board was sitting in the middle of the floor in the family room, its pieces scattered here and there. Alexus shook her head but said not a word. Vari noticed the head shake and immediately went to work putting the board game away.

"King's the one who did it," she muttered.

Alexus looked at King and pointed at the game. "Help your sister clean that up."

He pouted and crossed his arms over his chest.

"Don't make me say it again, King." Alexus gave him the look that said she wasn't messing around.

"Tamera," Rita said, stepping around to the front of the wheelchair, "go and get me a belt. It's about time for King to get some act-right in his life."

Suddenly King was all for putting away the game, especially when Tamera returned with the belt.

Alexus stood up for the first time since leaving the hospital and walked slowly to the sofa. It was an Italian leather sectional that she'd purchased in Ibiza, all white with gold stitching. She sat down and felt a hundred times better. The white sweat suit she had on was loose-fitting and just as comfy. QUEEN was written across the chest of the sweatshirt in large gold letters; it went perfectly with the sofa.

Rita turned on the television — an 80-inch smart TV— and turned to CNN.

Alexus was not surprised to see that the breaking news was all about her.

Don Lemon had the story, and he was milking it for all it was worth. 'Alexus Costilla is no longer in a coma, and she's also no longer in federal

custody. According to court documents obtained shortly after CNN cameras caught the American billionaire leaving the courthouse in Los Angeles, Alexus posted a forty-million-dollar bail and is due in court next month on charges of allegedly masterminding a Mexican drug cartel from right here in the US. Federal officials believe she inherited the notoriously violent cartel from her father when he passed away a few years ago after suffering a gunshot to the chest behind a northwest Indiana nightclub.

'The Costilla Cartel is believed to have made tens of billions of dollars smuggling kilos of cocaine and heroin into a number of countries, including the United States, Canada, and even as far away as the UK and Iceland. An informant alleges that Alexus and other higher-ranking members of the cartel were in cahoots with American politicians, judges, and numerous police departments and federal agencies.

'However, there has been a twist in the case. The main informant was found dead with a gunshot wound to the head several weeks ago. His body had been dumped in the Rio Grande. Apparently, he was the main source of information for the entire investigation. There have been no arrests or leads in his murder, but the informant's identity has been revealed, and he's none other than Flako Costilla, Alexus Costilla's uncle.

'Now the question looms: Was Alexus in any way connected to the death of her uncle? Some are saying yes, but there truly is no possible way she could have been involved in Flako Costilla's murder. She was already in a coma when federal agents arrested many of the Costilla Cartel's top echelon members, and he was dead by the time she came out of the coma early this morning...'

Alexus shook her head and rolled her eyes. I don't wanna hear this shit, she thought as Rita took a seat next to her.

"They're, uh, looking forward to you being in charge of things again," Rita said, obviously speaking of the members of Alexus's cartel. "Blake's been being the same old selfish Blake, you know. Your guys aren't feeling it."

"Have you talked to Mercedes?" Alexus drank more water. The ache in her throat was beginning to wane.

"Yeah. Yesterday."

Alexus frowned at her mother's terse reply. "Is something wrong?"

"She said she doesn't want anything more to do with us. Not while you're still in deep in what's going on here in Mexico. That suicide bombing terrified her."

"That bitch."

"Hey. Watch your mouth."

"I lost my husband taking up for her."

"Yeah, well, if you lost him, he didn't want to stay in the first place. Don't waste your time thinking about that mess. Like I told you, God will see you through this and a better man will come. You just focus on getting yourself together. Let go and let God. He's the only one I can guarantee will never let you down."

Alexus gritted her teeth together and pretended to find interest in what Don Lemon was saying.

A minute later Britney Bostic, Alexus's personal attorney, walked in with Dr. Melonie Farr, a psychologist who'd gone from operating an office in downtown Chicago to working full time with Alexus. The two women were Alexus's very best friends, though they strived to keep their relationships based solely on business.

"Britney," Alexus said, "I wanna be divorced from Blake by the end of the week. Also, I'd like you to phone Enrique at your earliest convenience and tell him to brutally murder every bitch Blake has stuck his dick in since I went into that coma."

Lock Down Publications and Ca$h Presents assisted publishing packages.

BASIC PACKAGE $499
Editing
Cover Design
Formatting

UPGRADED PACKAGE $800
Typing
Editing
Cover Design
Formatting

ADVANCE PACKAGE $1,200
Typing
Editing
Cover Design
Formatting
Copyright registration
Proofreading
Upload book to Amazon

LDP SUPREME PACKAGE $1,500
Typing
Editing
Cover Design
Formatting
Copyright registration
Proofreading
Set up Amazon account
Upload book to Amazon
Advertise on LDP Amazon and Facebook page

***Other services available upon request. Additional charges
may apply
Lock Down Publications
P.O. Box 944
Stockbridge, GA 30281-9998
Phone # 470 303-9761

Submission Guideline

Submit the first three chapters of your completed manuscript to ldpsubmissions@gmail.com, subject line:
Your book's title. The manuscript must be in a .doc file
and sent as an attachment. Document should be in
Times New Roman, double spaced and in size 12 font.
Also, provide your synopsis and full contact information. If sending multiple submissions, they must
each be in a separate email.

Have a story but no way to send it electronically? You
can still submit to LDP/Ca$h Presents. Send in the first
three chapters, written or typed, of your completed
manuscript to:

LDP: Submissions Dept
Po Box 944
Stockbridge, Ga 30281

*DO NOT send original manuscript. Must be a dupli-
cate.*

Provide your synopsis and a cover letter containing
your full contact information.

Thanks for considering LDP and Ca$h Presents.

NEW RELEASES

BORN IN THE GRAVE 3 by SELF MADE TAY

PROTÉGÉ OF A LEGEND 3 by COREY ROBINSON

GORILLAZ IN THE TRENCHES 2 by SAYNOMORE

BLOOD OF A GOON by ROMELL TUKES

THE COCAINE PRINCESS 8 by KING RIO

De'Kari

KINGPIN KILLAZ IV

STREET KINGS III

PAID IN BLOOD III

CARTEL KILLAZ IV

DOPE GODS III

Hood Rich

SINS OF A HUSTLA II

ASAD

YAYO V

Bred In The Game 2

S. Allen

THE STREETS WILL TALK II

By Yolanda Moore

SON OF A DOPE FIEND III

HEAVEN GOT A GHETTO III

SKI MASK MONEY III

By Renta

LOYALTY AIN'T PROMISED III

By Keith Williams

I'M NOTHING WITHOUT HIS LOVE II

SINS OF A THUG II

TO THE THUG I LOVED BEFORE II

IN A HUSTLER I TRUST II

By Monet Dragun

QUIET MONEY IV

EXTENDED CLIP III

THUG LIFE IV

By **Trai'Quan**

THE STREETS MADE ME IV

By **Larry D. Wright**

IF YOU CROSS ME ONCE III

King Rio

ANGEL V

By **Anthony Fields**

THE STREETS WILL NEVER CLOSE IV

By **K'ajji**

HARD AND RUTHLESS III

KILLA KOUNTY IV

By **Khufu**

MONEY GAME III

By **Smoove Dolla**

JACK BOYS VS DOPE BOYS IV

A GANGSTA'S QUR'AN V

COKE GIRLZ II

COKE BOYS II

LIFE OF A SAVAGE V

CHI'RAQ GANGSTAS V

SOSA GANG III

BRONX SAVAGES II

BODYMORE KINGPINS II

BLOOD OF A GOON II

By **Romell Tukes**

MURDA WAS THE CASE III

Elijah R. Freeman

AN UNFORESEEN LOVE IV

BABY, I'M WINTERTIME COLD III

By **Meesha**

QUEEN OF THE ZOO III

By **Black Migo**

CONFESSIONS OF A JACKBOY III

By **Nicholas Lock**

KING KILLA II

The Cocaine Princess 8

By Vincent "Vitto" Holloway
BETRAYAL OF A THUG III
By Fre$h
THE MURDER QUEENS III
By Michael Gallon
THE BIRTH OF A GANGSTER III
By Delmont Player
TREAL LOVE II
By Le'Monica Jackson
FOR THE LOVE OF BLOOD III
By Jamel Mitchell
RAN OFF ON DA PLUG II
By Paper Boi Rari
HOOD CONSIGLIERE III
By Keese
PRETTY GIRLS DO NASTY THINGS II
By Nicole Goosby
LOVE IN THE TRENCHES II
By Corey Robinson
IT'S JUST ME AND YOU II
By Ah'Million
FOREVER GANGSTA III
By Adrian Dulan
GORILLAZ IN THE TRENCHES III
By SayNoMore
THE COCAINE PRINCESS IX
By King Rio
CRIME BOSS II
Playa Ray
LOYALTY IS EVERYTHING III
Molotti
HERE TODAY GONE TOMORROW II

King Rio

By Fly Rock

REAL G'S MOVE IN SILENCE II

By Von Diesel

GRIMEY WAYS IV

By Ray Vinci

Available Now

RESTRAINING ORDER **I & II**

By **CA$H & Coffee**

LOVE KNOWS NO BOUNDARIES **I II & III**

By **Coffee**

RAISED AS A GOON I, II, III & IV

BRED BY THE SLUMS I, II, III

BLAST FOR ME I & II

ROTTEN TO THE CORE I II III

A BRONX TALE I, II, III

DUFFLE BAG CARTEL I II III IV V VI

HEARTLESS GOON I II III IV V

A SAVAGE DOPEBOY I II

DRUG LORDS I II III

CUTTHROAT MAFIA I II

KING OF THE TRENCHES

By **Ghost**

LAY IT DOWN **I & II**

LAST OF A DYING BREED I II

BLOOD STAINS OF A SHOTTA I & II III

The Cocaine Princess 8

By **Jamaica**

LOYAL TO THE GAME I II III

LIFE OF SIN I, II III

By **TJ & Jelissa**

BLOODY COMMAS I & II

SKI MASK CARTEL I II & III

KING OF NEW YORK I II,III IV V

RISE TO POWER I II III

COKE KINGS I II III IV V

BORN HEARTLESS I II III IV

KING OF THE TRAP I II

By **T.J. Edwards**

IF LOVING HIM IS WRONG...I & II

LOVE ME EVEN WHEN IT HURTS I II III

By **Jelissa**

WHEN THE STREETS CLAP BACK I & II III

THE HEART OF A SAVAGE I II III IV

MONEY MAFIA I II

LOYAL TO THE SOIL I II III

By **Jibril Williams**

A DISTINGUISHED THUG STOLE MY HEART I II & III

LOVE SHOULDN'T HURT I II III IV

RENEGADE BOYS I II III IV

PAID IN KARMA I II III

SAVAGE STORMS I II III

AN UNFORESEEN LOVE I II III

BABY, I'M WINTERTIME COLD I II

By **Meesha**

A GANGSTER'S CODE I &, II III

A GANGSTER'S SYN I II III

THE SAVAGE LIFE I II III

CHAINED TO THE STREETS I II III

189

King Rio

BLOOD ON THE MONEY I II III

A GANGSTA'S PAIN I II III

By J-Blunt

PUSH IT TO THE LIMIT

By **Bre' Hayes**

BLOOD OF A BOSS **I, II, III, IV, V**

SHADOWS OF THE GAME

TRAP BASTARD

By **Askari**

THE STREETS BLEED MURDER **I, II & III**

THE HEART OF A GANGSTA I II& III

By **Jerry Jackson**

CUM FOR ME I II III IV V VI VII VIII

An **LDP Erotica Collaboration**

BRIDE OF A HUSTLA **I II & II**

THE FETTI GIRLS **I, II& III**

CORRUPTED BY A GANGSTA I, II III, IV

BLINDED BY HIS LOVE

THE PRICE YOU PAY FOR LOVE I, II ,III

DOPE GIRL MAGIC I II III

By **Destiny Skai**

WHEN A GOOD GIRL GOES BAD

By **Adrienne**

THE COST OF LOYALTY I II III

By Kweli

A GANGSTER'S REVENGE **I II III & IV**

THE BOSS MAN'S DAUGHTERS I II III IV V

A SAVAGE LOVE **I & II**

BAE BELONGS TO ME I II

A HUSTLER'S DECEIT I, II, III

WHAT BAD BITCHES DO I, II, III

The Cocaine Princess 8

SOUL OF A MONSTER I II III
KILL ZONE
A DOPE BOY'S QUEEN I II III
TIL DEATH
By **Aryanna**
A KINGPIN'S AMBITON
A KINGPIN'S AMBITION **II**
I MURDER FOR THE DOUGH
By **Ambitious**
TRUE SAVAGE I II III IV V VI VII
DOPE BOY MAGIC I, II, III
MIDNIGHT CARTEL I II III
CITY OF KINGZ I II
NIGHTMARE ON SILENT AVE
THE PLUG OF LIL MEXICO II
CLASSIC CITY
By **Chris Green**
A DOPEBOY'S PRAYER
By **Eddie "Wolf" Lee**
THE KING CARTEL **I, II & III**
By **Frank Gresham**
THESE NIGGAS AIN'T LOYAL **I, II & III**
By **Nikki Tee**
GANGSTA SHYT **I II &III**
By **CATO**
THE ULTIMATE BETRAYAL
By **Phoenix**
BOSS'N UP **I , II & III**
By **Royal Nicole**
I LOVE YOU TO DEATH
By **Destiny J**
I RIDE FOR MY HITTA

King Rio

I STILL RIDE FOR MY HITTA
By **Misty Holt**
LOVE & CHASIN' PAPER
By **Qay Crockett**
TO DIE IN VAIN
SINS OF A HUSTLA
By **ASAD**
BROOKLYN HUSTLAZ
By **Boogsy Morina**
BROOKLYN ON LOCK I & II
By **Sonovia**
GANGSTA CITY
By **Teddy Duke**
A DRUG KING AND HIS DIAMOND I & II III
A DOPEMAN'S RICHES
HER MAN, MINE'S TOO I, II
CASH MONEY HO'S
THE WIFEY I USED TO BE I II
PRETTY GIRLS DO NASTY THINGS
By Nicole Goosby
TRAPHOUSE KING **I II & III**
KINGPIN KILLAZ I II III
STREET KINGS I II
PAID IN BLOOD **I II**
CARTEL KILLAZ I II III
DOPE GODS I II
By **Hood Rich**
LIPSTICK KILLAH **I, II, III**
CRIME OF PASSION I II & III
FRIEND OR FOE I II III
By **Mimi**

The Cocaine Princess 8

STEADY MOBBN' **I, II, III**

THE STREETS STAINED MY SOUL I II III

By **Marcellus Allen**

WHO SHOT YA **I, II, III**

SON OF A DOPE FIEND I II

HEAVEN GOT A GHETTO I II

SKI MASK MONEY I II

Renta

GORILLAZ IN THE BAY **I II III IV**

TEARS OF A GANGSTA I II

3X KRAZY I II

STRAIGHT BEAST MODE I II

DE'KARI

TRIGGADALE I II III

MURDAROBER WAS THE CASE I II

Elijah R. Freeman

GOD BLESS THE TRAPPERS I, II, III

THESE SCANDALOUS STREETS I, II, III

FEAR MY GANGSTA I, II, III IV, V

THESE STREETS DON'T LOVE NOBODY I, II

BURY ME A G I, II, III, IV, V

A GANGSTA'S EMPIRE I, II, III, IV

THE DOPEMAN'S BODYGAURD I II

THE REALEST KILLAZ I II III

THE LAST OF THE OGS I II III

Tranay Adams

THE STREETS ARE CALLING

Duquie Wilson

MARRIED TO A BOSS I II III

By **Destiny Skai & Chris Green**

KINGZ OF THE GAME I II III IV V VI VII

CRIME BOSS

193

King Rio

Playa Ray
SLAUGHTER GANG I II III
RUTHLESS HEART I II III
By Willie Slaughter
FUK SHYT
By Blakk Diamond
DON'T F#CK WITH MY HEART I II
By Linnea
ADDICTED TO THE DRAMA I II III
IN THE ARM OF HIS BOSS II
By Jamila
YAYO I II III IV
A SHOOTER'S AMBITION I II
BRED IN THE GAME
By S. Allen
TRAP GOD I II III
RICH $AVAGE I II III
MONEY IN THE GRAVE I II III
By Martell Troublesome Bolden
FOREVER GANGSTA I II
GLOCKS ON SATIN SHEETS I II
By Adrian Dulan
TOE TAGZ I II III IV
LEVELS TO THIS SHYT I II
IT'S JUST ME AND YOU
By Ah'Million
KINGPIN DREAMS I II III
RAN OFF ON DA PLUG
By Paper Boi Rari
CONFESSIONS OF A GANGSTA I II III IV
CONFESSIONS OF A JACKBOY I II

The Cocaine Princess 8

By Nicholas Lock

I'M NOTHING WITHOUT HIS LOVE

SINS OF A THUG

TO THE THUG I LOVED BEFORE

A GANGSTA SAVED XMAS

IN A HUSTLER I TRUST

By Monet Dragun

CAUGHT UP IN THE LIFE I II III

THE STREETS NEVER LET GO I II III

By Robert Baptiste

NEW TO THE GAME I II III

MONEY, MURDER & MEMORIES I II III

By **Malik D. Rice**

LIFE OF A SAVAGE I II III IV

A GANGSTA'S QUR'AN I II III IV

MURDA SEASON I II III

GANGLAND CARTEL I II III

CHI'RAQ GANGSTAS I II III IV

KILLERS ON ELM STREET I II III

JACK BOYZ N DA BRONX I II III

A DOPEBOY'S DREAM I II III

JACK BOYS VS DOPE BOYS I II III

COKE GIRLZ

COKE BOYS

SOSA GANG I II

BRONX SAVAGES

BODYMORE KINGPINS

BLOOD OF A GOON

By Romell Tukes

LOYALTY AIN'T PROMISED I II

By Keith Williams

QUIET MONEY I II III

King Rio

THUG LIFE I II III

EXTENDED CLIP I II

A GANGSTA'S PARADISE

By **Trai'Quan**

THE STREETS MADE ME I II III

By **Larry D. Wright**

THE ULTIMATE SACRIFICE I, II, III, IV, V, VI

KHADIFI

IF YOU CROSS ME ONCE I II

ANGEL I II III IV

IN THE BLINK OF AN EYE

By **Anthony Fields**

THE LIFE OF A HOOD STAR

By **Ca$h & Rashia Wilson**

THE STREETS WILL NEVER CLOSE I II III

By **K'ajji**

CREAM I II III

THE STREETS WILL TALK

By **Yolanda Moore**

NIGHTMARES OF A HUSTLA I II III

By **King Dream**

CONCRETE KILLA I II III

VICIOUS LOYALTY I II III

By **Kingpen**

HARD AND RUTHLESS I II

MOB TOWN 251

THE BILLIONAIRE BENTLEYS I II III

REAL G'S MOVE IN SILENCE

By **Von Diesel**

GHOST MOB

Stilloan Robinson

The Cocaine Princess 8

MOB TIES I II III IV V VI

SOUL OF A HUSTLER, HEART OF A KILLER I II

GORILLAZ IN THE TRENCHES I II

By SayNoMore

BODYMORE MURDERLAND I II III

THE BIRTH OF A GANGSTER I II

By Delmont Player

FOR THE LOVE OF A BOSS

By C. D. Blue

MOB$ED UP I II III IV

THE BRICK MAN I II III IV V

THE COCAINE PRINCESS I II III IV V VI VII VIII

By King Rio

KILLA KOUNTY I II III IV

By Khufu

MONEY GAME I II

By Smoove Dolla

A GANGSTA'S KARMA I II III

By FLAME

KING OF THE TRENCHES I II III

by **GHOST & TRANAY ADAMS**

QUEEN OF THE ZOO I II

By **Black Migo**

GRIMEY WAYS I II III

By Ray Vinci

XMAS WITH AN ATL SHOOTER

By Ca$h & Destiny Skai

KING KILLA

By Vincent "Vitto" Holloway

BETRAYAL OF A THUG I II

By Fre$h

THE MURDER QUEENS I II

King Rio

By Michael Gallon

TREAL LOVE

By Le'Monica Jackson

FOR THE LOVE OF BLOOD I II

By Jamel Mitchell

HOOD CONSIGLIERE I II

By Keese

PROTÉGÉ OF A LEGEND I II III

LOVE IN THE TRENCHES

By Corey Robinson

BORN IN THE GRAVE I II III

By Self Made Tay

MOAN IN MY MOUTH

By XTASY

TORN BETWEEN A GANGSTER AND A GENTLEMAN

By J-BLUNT & Miss Kim

LOYALTY IS EVERYTHING I II

Molotti

HERE TODAY GONE TOMORROW

By Fly Rock

PILLOW PRINCESS

By S. Hawkins

NAÏVE TO THE STREETS

WOMEN LIE MEN LIE I II III

GIRLS FALL LIKE DOMINOS

STACK BEFORE YOU SPURLGE

By A. Roy Milligan

<u>BOOKS BY LDP'S CEO, CA$H</u>

TRUST IN NO MAN

TRUST IN NO MAN 2

TRUST IN NO MAN 3

BONDED BY BLOOD

SHORTY GOT A THUG

THUGS CRY

THUGS CRY 2

THUGS CRY 3

TRUST NO BITCH

TRUST NO BITCH 2

TRUST NO BITCH 3

TIL MY CASKET DROPS

RESTRAINING ORDER

RESTRAINING ORDER 2

IN LOVE WITH A CONVICT

LIFE OF A HOOD STAR

XMAS WITH AN ATL SHOOTER

King Rio